PENGUIN

ROMANTIC FAIRY TALES

JOHANN WOLFGANG VON GOETHE was bo nkfurt am Main in 1749. At twenty-four he wrote *Götz von Berlichingen*, a play which established him at the forefront of the 'Storm and Stress' movement. *Werther*, a novel, was even greater success. Goethe then began work on *Faust* and on *Egmont*, another tragedy. His friendship with Schiller proved another source of inspiration, and he published regularly until his death. The most notable of Goethe's later achievements were *Wilhem Meister* and *Elective Affinities*, and, in drama, the second part of *Faust*. He died in 1832, soon after completing *Faust*.

LUDWIG TIECK was born in Berlin in 1773. He wrote a number of successful works for the stage, including *Puss in Boots* (1797), *Blue Beard* (1797) and *Prinz Zerbino* (1799), as well as romantic stories such as *Eckbert the Fair* (1797). Early success was followed by the supernatural horror story *The Rune Mountain* (1804), and works of more social and historical realism. Tieck was involved in August Wilhelm Schlegel's translation of the works of Shakespeare (1797–1810), and also translated Cervantes's *Don Quixote* (1799–1804). He died in 1853.

FRIEDRICH DE LA MOTTE FOUQUÉ was born into an old Norman noble family in 1777. The son of a Prussian general, he himself served in the Prussian military for a number of years. He died in Berlin in 1843. Fouqué published widely in poetry, prose fiction and drama. He is best known for his prose romances, which were based on sources such as Old French poems and Norse mythology, the most famous of which is the fairy tale *Undine* (1811).

CLEMENS BRENTANO (1778–1842) was a member of a group of Romantic writers in Heidelberg who were influenced by German fairy tales and folklore. The highly expressive tendencies of this movement, however, had far-reaching consequences for Brentano, who later devoted himself to religion, becoming a Roman Catholic in 1818 and retreating to a monastery for six years. His works are considered to be some of the finest examples of Romantic *Märchen*, or fairy tales, especially his prose narratives such as *The Tale of Honest Casper and Fair Annie* (1817).

CAROL TULLY was born in 1968 in Galashiels, Scotland. After gaining a BA from the University of Strathclyde, she went on to take her PhD at Queen Mary and Westfield College, London. Before taking up her current post as lecturer in German at the University of Wales Bangor, she taught at King's College, London and the University of Leeds. As well as writing on nineteenth-century women's literature in Germany, Carol Tully is the author of *Creating a National Identity: A Comparative Study of German and Spanish Romanticism* (Stuttgart, 1997).

Romantic Fairy Tales

Translated and edited by
CAROL TULLY

PENGUIN BOOKS

PENGUIN BOOKS

Published by the Penguin Group
Penguin Books Ltd, 27 Wrights Lane, London w8 5TZ, England
Penguin Putnam Inc., 375 Hudson Street, New York, New York 10014, USA
Penguin Books Australia Ltd, Ringwood, Victoria, Australia
Penguin Books Canada Ltd, 10 Alcorn Avenue, Toronto, Ontario, Canada M4V 3B2
Penguin Books (NZ) Ltd, Private Bag 102902, NSMC, Auckland, New Zealand

Penguin Books Ltd, Registered Offices: Harmondsworth, Middlesex, England

This translation first published 2000
1 3 5 7 9 10 8 6 4 2

Set in 10/12.5 pt Monotype Baskerville
Typeset by Rowland Phototypesetting Ltd, Bury St Edmunds, Suffolk
Printed in England by Clays Ltd, St Ives plc

CONTENTS

ACKNOWLEDGEMENTS

I would like to express my grateful thanks to Professor Tony Harper of the University of Strathclyde for taking such a keen interest in this anthology. His comments, suggestions and infinite patience have been invaluable at every stage of the project. I would particularly like to thank him for the verse translations in Tieck's *Eckbert the Fair*, which are entirely his.

I would also like to thank Professor Jeremy Adler of King's College, University of London, for encouraging me to undertake this project and for so generously giving of his time to offer advice on the Introduction.

INTRODUCTION

German Romanticism and the Fairy Tale

The Romantic period in Germany, which roughly spans the years from 1795 to 1820, is critically acknowledged as one of the finest periods in German literature. Writers of the time include some of those best known in the German canon whose work still carries resonance for us some two hundred years later. The mood of the period very much reflects the turmoil of an age of upheaval and change – an age of revolution, of war in Europe, of intellectual and scientific discovery – which witnessed a change in the balance of society, the legacy of which still confronts us today. This pivotal period in the development of European society saw the demise of the vestiges of feudalism; old certainties and enlightened reason were questioned simultaneously as a new social order began to emerge.

The literary response to this age of extremes was no less contradictory, seeking both the comfort and security of the past, yet also fostering the spirit of innovation. It is hardly surprising, then, to find that the Romantic movement in Germany is itself in many ways a contradiction, neither homogenous nor easily defined. This, combined with a marked individuality, which sets the movement apart from the British or French schools, makes German Romanticism notoriously difficult to categorize in simple terms. Indeed, its principles were often misunderstood or only partially appreciated in its time. A preoccupation with the self and a critical stance towards the Enlightenment and Neo-Classicism meant that contemporary reception was not always kind. Goethe once pronounced: 'Romanticism is a disease, Classicism is health.' Others were less condemnatory, Heine perhaps approaching the clearest understanding: 'Classic art portrays the finite, romantic art also suggests the infinite.' Nevertheless, Heine too went on to openly criticize what he saw to be the degenerate nature of the school.

Contemporary society found it difficult to cope with Romanticism's uncomfortable tendency to centre on the *Nachtseite*, 'the darker side' of human existence, the inexplicable self that Enlightenment had sought to force towards the light of day. The Romantic mind revelled in the unknown, the uncanny, and actively pursued relations with a nebulous past filled with indefinite and infinite possibilities – not least, the mysterious world of the fairy tale.

The fairy tale appealed to writers involved in the movement throughout its duration. Both *Frühromantik* (early Romanticism) and *Hochromantik* (High Romanticism) share many similar ideals and display similar trends, but there is a difference in emphasis that is worth outlining as it is reflected in the texts presented here. The aesthetics of the earlier period were largely based around the critical theories of the brothers Friedrich (1772–1829) and August Wilhelm Schlegel (1767–1845), whose periodical, the *Athenaeum* (1798–1800), became a forum for the discussion of literature and aesthetics. Other key figures in this close group, who met and worked in Jena, were Friedrich von Hardenberg, known as Novalis (1772–1801), Ludwig Tieck (1773–1853) and Wilhelm Heinrich Wackenroder (1773–98). The central premise of early Romantic aesthetic theory was the creation of what Friedrich Schlegel termed *Universalpoesie* – the fusion of the poetic genres with philosophy, criticism and rhetoric to form a continually developing aesthetic ideal. In shaping the concept of 'universal poetry', Schlegel sought to achieve infinite perfectibility through a synthesis of contrary forms. This aesthetic vision owed much to mysticism and understood art as a vehicle for the symbolic expression of the transcendental as perceived by the imagination of the artist. Texts like Tieck's *Der blonde Eckbert* (*Eckbert the Fair*, 1797), in this volume, and Novalis's *Die Lehrlinge zu Saïs* (*The Disciples at Saïs*, 1802) are typical of this early period in their use of pantheist imagery, symbolism, and the depiction of the artist as the embodiment of the Romantic self. This appreciation of the *Nachtseite*, of Nature and the organic, is a direct response to the perceived sterility of Enlightenment aesthetic theory with its reliance on reason and

Neo-Classical order. It was precisely this tendency that led to criticism of Romanticism in its early years but which also enabled its continued survival as a force for literary and philosophical innovation.

With the Romantic ideal firmly established in mainstream intellectual debate by the end of the first decade of the nineteenth century, the preoccupation during the later period was less the theoretical discussion of aesthetics and philosophy than the role of the supernatural and a growing fascination for the past, particularly as expressed in folk culture. Among the most prominent writers of the later period were Achim von Arnim (1781–1831), Clemens Brentano (1778–1842) and Joseph von Eichendorff (1788–1857), all living and working in Heidelberg. Brentano later joined the group of writers in Berlin that included E. T. A. Hoffmann (1776–1822) and Friedrich de la Motte Fouqué (1777–1843). A key area of interest for these later groups, which in many ways encapsulates the contradictory nature of the movement with its fascination for both past and future, was the development of new scientific ideas such as mesmerism and magnetism. This is particularly clear in the work of E. T. A. Hoffmann in texts such as *Der Sandmann* (*The Sandman*, 1815). The unconscious workings of the human mind and body seemed to complement existing interest in the *Nachtseite* as rational explanation stood open to question in the face of scientific doubt. Despite the best efforts of Enlightenment, the supernatural still maintained the upper hand. The fusing of this interest in the uncanny with an idealization of the past, particularly the Middle Ages, fitted well with the wider Romantic world view as efforts were made to revive and record aspects of ancient Germanic culture, a preoccupation that in turn inspired the development of modern literary genres. This tendency embodied the growing Romantic desire to see a revival of German culture, which was in itself a response to the difficult political situation of the later Napoleonic period. In this respect, the later Romantics took up the interests of the late eighteenth-century *Sturm-und-Drang* ('Storm-and-Stress') movement and were heavily influenced by the work of the philosopher and critic, Johann Gottfried Herder (1744–1803). Fouqué's *Undine* (1811), in this volume, is typical of the period in its apotheosis of the medieval world and reliance on the tropes and symbolism of Germanic legend. This was the source of an identifiable, specifically German identity, which many felt had been denied by the French cultural domination during the late seventeenth and eighteenth centuries. The Romantic self, the artist, gained a counterpart, the national self – the Romantic spirit of the German nation.

This fascination for the past encouraged certain genres that reflect the aesthetic preferences of the movement as a whole. Drama, the corner-stone of Classicism, is far less in evidence, yet the lyric continues to play a key role. Mirroring British Romantic trends, much German Romantic poetry was inspired by the simplicity of the traditional ballad, as collected by Arnim and Brentano in *Des Knaben Wunderhorn* (*The Boy's Magic Horn*, 1808). The *Novelle* also consolidated its central role in German literature at this time, following interest in early collections such as Boccaccio's *The Decameron* (1352) and Cervantes' *Novelas ejemplares* (1613). The most notable collections are Arnim's *Der Wintergarten* (*The Winter Garden*, 1809), Tieck's *Phantasus* (1812–17) and E. T. A. Hoffmann's *Die Serapionsbrüder* (*The Brothers Serapion*, 1819). Yet perhaps the most representative of the central Romantic genres is that featured in this volume – the *Kunstmärchen* or literary fairy tale.

Literally, the term *Märchen* means 'little tale' or 'short story', but it has particular association with tales of wondrous events, found universally in oral culture, and generally given in English translation as 'fairy tale' or 'folk tale'. The notion of the fairy tale is one that appeals to us all. The very word conjures up images of the struggle between good and evil, of knights, princesses and wonderful creatures possessing powers beyond the grasp of human understanding. The almost inevitable association of the genre with childhood is, however, a product of the modern age and does not reflect the true breadth of significance these often complex narratives have to offer as cultural ciphers. The value of the genre to literature in general and to German Romanticism in particular is immense. Ironically, given the general hostility towards French culture during the Napoleonic period, the popularity of the traditional German folk tale or *Märchen* among the German Romantics stems from the popularization of the *conte de fées* in France during the seventeenth and eighteenth centuries through collections such as Madame d'Aulnoy's *Contes des Fées* (*Fairy Tales*, 1698) and Charles Perrault's *Contes de ma Mère l'Oye* (*Tales of Mother Goose*, 1697). The genre, in its simplest form, can be described relatively briefly as a tale of limited length that involves certain types and motifs, such as the quest and the trial. The setting is an unreal world filled with fantastic characters and locations and involving the 'marvellous' along with a measure of wish fulfilment. It is hardly surprising to find the 'marvellous' *Märchen* to be of interest to artists and writers alike, even when traditional oral culture was out of vogue. Even the rational mind of the German Enlightenment found a use for the fairy tale as a means to transmit a didactic message, intended to educate and entertain, but always within the clearly defined boundaries of acknowledged artifice, boundaries that the *Kunstmärchen* often strives to ignore. Subsequent interest in the so-called 'natural' form of the genre, the *Volksmärchen*, surfaced as part of the general revival of traditional oral culture inspired by the work of Herder and others in the late eighteenth century and resulted in the publication of an array of collections including Johann Musäus's *Volksmärchen der Deutschen* (*German Folk Tales*, 1782–6). This interest continued into the Romantic period, promoted by the work of figures central to the early development of the movement such as Novalis and Tieck. Perhaps the most famous collection of all, the *Kinder- und Hausmärchen* (*Children's and Household Tales*) of the Brothers Grimm (Jacob, 1785–1863; and Wilhelm, 1786–1859), was compiled during the later period and first published in 1812. This was an enormous success, which was expanded and elaborated during the brothers' lifetime and for many readers came to represent the voice of the German people. Yet, interest in the fairy-tale genre was not confined to the recording and reviving of ancient Germanic culture, it also provided an invaluable resource that was particularly suited to the expression of the new Romantic aesthetic, given its inherent ability to communicate literary innovation, spiritual aspiration, psychological insight, and a social ideal with equal clarity.

The *Kunstmärchen*, to use an admittedly arguable term (the Romantics referred to their tales simply as *Märchen*), is a specifically literary branch of the *Märchen* genre. The term means 'literary fairy tale' and refers to texts created to simulate or evoke folk tales. This is in opposition to the *Volksmärchen* that claims to originate from the 'people' themselves.

The *Kunstmärchen* is closely related to the *Volksmärchen*, particularly in terms of content, yet also owes a debt to the *Fabel* and the *Novelle* in its often didactic aim, its use of concentrated narrative, and its limited length. However, the *Kunstmärchen* differs from the *Novelle* in one vital respect: its frame of social reference. Martin Swales, in his study of the *Novelle*, points to the fact that the *Wendepunkt* (central event/ turning-point), a main characteristic of the genre, 'is marginal to the broad generality of ordered social experience, but it is not located in a separate world' (*The German Novelle*, p. 33). The *Kunstmärchen*, however, is very much located in a separate world, thus allowing the author to portray social ideals in a symbolic setting by exploiting both *Volksmärchen* conventions and the ideals of the Romantic aesthetic. The typical plot revolves around the overcoming of some difficulty, be it a struggle against evil or a task that requires completion. Polar opposites such as illness/cure, capture/escape, and so on, are also commonly found. There are various themes, tropes and symbols that are borrowed directly from oral literature and incorporated into the literary texts, such as colours, metals and minerals as well as extremes and contrasts. Certain types of character are also transferred from the *Volks-* to the *Kunstmärchen*, such as testers, helpers and contrasting characters. However, whereas the *Volksmärchen* character is rarely given particular individuality, the hero of the *Kunstmärchen* may be given more psychological depth. The style of the *Volksmärchen* is that of a concentrated narrative that divulges only the most necessary information. The *Kunstmärchen*, however, tends towards descriptions of natural surroundings, poetic interludes and emotive reactions. As a result, the *Volksmärchen* usually produces a far clearer, simpler narrative of the type necessary for oral presentation. This contrasts greatly with the ambiguity and complexity often found in its literary counterpart. For example, while often employing the notion of polarity found in the extremes and contrasts of the *Volksmärchen*, the *Kunstmärchen* does not always complete the standard fairy-tale formula: where there is desire, there may not be fulfilment; where there is a problem, there may not necessarily be a solution. In this respect, the Romantic *Kunstmärchen* reflects the general mood of the post-1789 period by questioning the rationality of the Enlightenment, and its claimed omniscience. It is this critical aspect that renders the genre so vital to the development of the Romantic movement in Germany.

The tales chosen for this volume reflect the development of the genre from Weimar Classicism to the final years of the later Romantic school. The pre-Romantic allegory of Goethe's *The Fairy Tale* is succeeded by Tieck's uncanny archetypal fantasy, *Eckbert the Fair*, so indicative of the early Romantic period. This is then developed with a flourish in Fouqué's highly stylized celebration of the idealized medieval world, *Undine*. Finally, emphasizing close links with the *Novelle*, Brentano's *The Tale of Honest Casper and Fair Annie* retains its folk-tale elements while adhering to the norms of the *Novelle* genre. Each text can be seen to epitomize the *Kunstmärchen* genre at a different stage in its own development and that of the Romantic movement itself.

Johann Wolfgang von Goethe – *The Fairy Tale*

Johann Wolfgang von Goethe (1749–1832) needs little introduction; the acknowledged colossus of German literature, his influence, not least that which he exerted on his contemporaries, is immeasurable. Ever the adversary of the Romantic school, Goethe would no doubt be rather surprised to find his work included in an anthology of German Romantic texts, but *The Fairy Tale* was seminal to the development of the *Kunstmärchen* genre and also encapsulates the aesthetic transition from Classicism to Romanticism at the end of the eighteenth century. The tale was written in the late summer of 1795 and appeared in the October edition of Schiller's literary periodical *Die Horen* (*The Hours*), closing the cycle of *Unterhaltungen Deutscher Ausgewanderten* (*Conversations of German Emigrants*).

Mythical and Classical allusions abound in this complex text. The plot is both intricate and ethereal with the supernatural clearly in evidence. The tale unfolds to reveal both prophecy and resurrection as the many characters unite in a mystical ritual that sees the coming of a new age. The setting, although described in detail, retains the mystique of irreality; a river divides the beautiful East from an inhospitable West and flows above an awe-inspiring subterranean realm. We are introduced to each of the characters in turn as their mutual need for interaction is made clear. First of all we encounter the ferryman, one of the few empowered to cross the river independently and take others with him. He ferries the two will-o'-the-wisps to the other side where they encounter the serpent. She is also able to span the river, transforming herself into an elegant bridge. The curious serpent then leads us to the underground realm of the four metal kings who patiently await the new dawn in their cavernous temple. In the temple we are introduced to the man with the lamp, another figure whose powers are key to the realization of the prophecy. His wife functions as a go-between and leads us to the two remaining key figures, the young knight and beautiful Lily, whose sublime union will preside over the new era when it finally dawns. These characters need to work in unison but are variously possessed of special characteristics or objects that are absurd and foster isolation. The vivacity of the two will-o'-the-wisps sparks traffic between the two zones, as a result of which various figures are brought together to herald the new era. The value of the stability this will bring is represented by the young king who embodies wisdom, beauty and power in harmony and who has been educated by the power of love. The symbols of the joyful new era are the temple, the spiritual source, which rises from the depths to dominate the landscape, and the bridge created by the serpent, which spans the river and is the basis for trade and friendly relations: an allegorical representation of the desire for European stability.

The tale incorporates the fairy-tale goal of recovering order from chaos and links fairy-tale motifs such as magical powers, metamorphosis and numeric formulae with tropes more common to the legend such as dynastic order and the inorganic world. The Utopia created brings the social and the aesthetic together to create a counter-image to the terror of the French Revolution, highlighted by the morality that is central to the text. Self-sacrifice is necessary for the common good, thus infusing this Romantic dream world with an idealization of lofty reason. Visual imagery is central – light plays a key role as does colour; motion is also important – buildings move and creatures are transformed into structures. The personification of objects and minerals is also key. However, the use of these various elements is at times inconsistent. Allegorical images such as the serpent forming a circle and the four metal kings are given no real explanation whereas the serpent's metamorphosis into the bridge is clearly a symbol of progress. Such inconsistencies add to the often impenetrable complexity of the text, making the tale difficult to interpret. Goethe was himself far from forthcoming, saying it was meant to be seen in symbolic rather than allegorical terms but offering no further explanation. Despite the emphasis on the marvellous and the fantastic, the tale still displays the coolness of Classicism while clearly indulging individual imagination, the corner-stone of Romanticism; the play of the imagination is unhindered by the laws of reality but nevertheless dependent on intellect. The style is serious and factually descriptive with elements of solemnity, and the tone is consistent throughout with no concession to the eighteenth-century fairy tale, which alluded to the irreality of the text. This strange realm is described as if it were quite familiar – a semi-dream world inhabited by people, spirits and animals with no boundaries to the inorganic, a trait that enables a merging of all elements in what is essentially a thoroughly Romantic synthesis.

Ludwig Tieck – *Eckbert the Fair*

Ludwig Tieck (1773–1853), though undoubtedly one of the leading figures of the Romantic movement, produced a range of work during his long life that covers far more than a single style of German literature and more than one genre. His later literary works belong rather more to the realist mode, and his influential work as a translator of Cervantes and Shakespeare is still highly valued today.

His fairy tale, *Eckbert the Fair*, appeared in 1797 in his collection of *Volksmärchen* and was later included in the *Phantasus* collection of 1812–17. The tale is one of his best-known works and is readily acknowledged as one of the central texts of German Romanticism. The piece is sometimes classified as a *Novelle* but bears all the hallmarks of the literary fairy tale. Tieck's inspiration for this tale was not only the

Volksmärchen, but also the traditional German *Volksbuch* or chap-book, reflecting his wider interest in ancient Germanic culture. There is also evidence of his growing fascination with the work of the Protestant mystic, Jakob Böhme, which is further developed in the later sister tale, *Der Runenberg* (*The Rune Mountain*, 1802). Both works are considered representative of the early Romantic school.

This tale within a tale tells of the demise of a young couple, Eckbert and Bertha, upon opening their home and hearts to Eckbert's friend, Walther. Yet the cause of their subsequent misery has less to do with their guest than the hidden truths of the past. The inner narrative relates the childhood experiences of Bertha. She tells how she left the home of her impoverished parents and eventually found her way to an idyllic life in the lonely woods with an old woman, her dog, and her magic bird. After a period of peaceful existence, Bertha becomes dissatisfied, steals the magic bird and makes her way back to the outside world. Here she finds it hard to cope with the harsh realities of life and with her own guilty conscience. Eventually, endowed with the riches given her by the magic bird, she kills the poor creature and marries Eckbert. Having told this tale to Walther, she is horrified to discover that he can remember the name of the old woman's dog, something she has not been able to do. The paranoia that this causes becomes the focus for the outer narrative as both she and Eckbert are driven to their doom, guilt-ridden and in fear of insanity. The end of the tale reveals the depths to which they have sunk both morally and in terms of their own understanding of reality as the old woman reveals their true relationship as brother and sister.

The tale differs from the traditional fairy tale not merely because of its unhappy ending – many of the Grimms' tales, for example, have less than fortunate outcomes – but rather through the transcendence of two varying levels of perception. Initially, at least, mundane reality and the fairy-tale world seem to be clearly divided, until, that is, Walther's response to Bertha's tale causes the two worlds to encroach on one another, finally fusing in Eckbert's madness. No explanation is offered for the events as they occur in either world and the tale ends in mystery and terror, reflecting the Romantic preoccupation with the *Nachtseite*. *Waldeinsamkeit*, 'the solitude of the lonely woods', represents both Romantic enchantment and demonic chaos, the latter played out in the minds of the unfortunate protagonists. This psychological element plays an important role. The transcendence of the two levels of perception is essentially psychological, as is the motivation for Bertha's childish dreams of escaping poverty. She finds solace in the isolated idyll of the lonely woods until the idyll too becomes mundane routine, whereupon she is once more dissatisfied and longs for another life. Eckbert's demise is also psychological as he commits murder to free himself from the fear of a confidant to a hidden secret. The end of the tale reveals incest as a symbol for self-imposed isolation from society. This treatment of the failings of humanity criticizes individual and collective alike – the Romantic self is found wanting in a depraved world crying out for revitalization.

Friedrich de la Motte Fouqué – *Undine*

Friedrich de la Motte Fouqué (1777–1843) came from an old Norman noble family, forced into exile after the Edict of Nantes. His literary career began in 1802 after a short spell in the military. He published in all genres and was heavily influenced by the Schlegel brothers, August Wilhelm in particular. *Undine* first appeared in 1811 as the *Frühlingsheft* (Spring Volume) of the literary journal, *Jahreszeiten* (*The Seasons*), for which Fouqué was the editor and sole contributor. The tale made the author's name and appealed to a wide audience, requiring a second edition in its first year. Its success inspired a number of adaptations including an opera by E. T. A. Hoffmann, first performed in Berlin in 1816.

Undine is in many ways the ultimate *Kunstmärchen*. The longest in the present volume, the text offers a myriad of fairy-tale elements, combined with a complex plot and ethereal atmosphere. The tale centres on the fate of the main protagonist, the water nymph, Undine. This charming, beautiful creature finds herself the ward of two lowly fisherfolk. Her stable, if rather moody, existence is thrown into turmoil by the arrival of the knight Huldbrand, with whom she immediately falls in love. Undine knows that in order to gain a soul and attain true human emotion she must marry a man who loves her as much as she loves him and who will never betray her. Any fall from grace on his part would end in certain disaster as the unfortunate girl would then be reclaimed by the elements and doomed to a life of misery, bereft of human contact. Once the couple marry all seems set to continue as it should but for the appearance of Bertalda, the true daughter of the fisherfolk, who has been adopted by a wealthy family. Huldbrand finds himself torn between the two women, which, combined with the persistent efforts of Undine's evil uncle Kühleborn, eventually leads to the disastrous outcome so feared by Undine. Huldbrand's infidelity is finally punished in a moving finale where Undine herself is forced to kill him at the behest of her elemental family, a request she is sadly powerless to refuse.

This powerful tale owes its inspiration to a number of sources including Fouqué's own private love life. Literary influences are clearly the medieval ballad and the world of medieval legend. Huldbrand is the archetypal benevolent knight and the world he inhabits typifies the idealized Germanic Middle Ages so central to the Romantic understanding of German culture. Undine's elemental world combines the chap-book legend of Melusine with the writings of Paracelsus in his *Liber de nymphis, sylphis, pygmaeis et salamandris et de caeteris spiritibus* (1591). Both sources were later explored by Brentano in his post-humously published collection of *Rheinmärchen* (written 1816; published 1846). Nature and the *Nachtseite* are fused in the figure of Undine herself. This once untroubled, moody child of Nature becomes a loving, suffering woman and soon discovers that such suffering equates with the possession of a human soul. Reality and the supernatural are further fused through the antics of Kühleborn, who remains on the periphery of the real world yet acts upon it with devastating consequences. His manifold manifestations are wholly tangible – a soaking waterfall, a fountain master, a stream – yet there are no means to stop or control him as he moves from one level to the next, ever bound to his source element of water. The emotional shortcomings of humanity are demonstrated in Huldbrand's failure to love Undine adequately and his fickle desire for gratification. His troubled attempts to come to terms with his wife's unusual kin represent the inability of the human mind to fully grasp the mysteries of Nature, the infinitely incomprehensible, and show the vulnerability of humanity in a world where reason has no bearing. In this respect, the *Kunstmärchen* can once again be seen to reflect the wider philosophical debate of the period.

Clemens Brentano – *The Tale of Honest Casper and Fair Annie*

Clemens Brentano (1778–1842) was a genial but complex character, in many ways insecure and at times demanding of his friends, in particular his fellow-writer Achim von Arnim. His early literary leanings later gave way to a religious fervour that preoccupied his mind for the rest of his days. *The Tale of Honest Casper and Fair Annie* was one of the last works he wrote while in Berlin in 1817 and in many ways reflects his spiritual struggle in its questioning of life, faith and morality.

The tale is the tragic depiction of the folly of false honour. The inner narrative tells of the fate of a young couple, Honest Casper and Fair Annie, both doomed to be destroyed by a false understanding of honour. Casper, a proud young soldier, is driven to suicide after discovering the immoral ways of his father and brother, whereas Annie, having been betrayed by her noble lover, kills her own child and is then tried for infanticide. The outer narrative tells of the efforts of Annie's godmother, Casper's grandmother, to have the couple buried together in an honourable grave. She is assisted in her quest by the narrator, the unnamed writer. The tragedy is heightened by the grandmother, who, despite her great age, faith and resignation, adheres to the same sense of false honour that has claimed both young people's lives.

The tale has a complex narrative structure, which undoubtedly owes more to the *Novelle* genre than to the fairy tale. There is much in the text that foreshadows a more realist tone, particularly the temporal setting, which, unlike the other texts in this volume, is clearly contemporary, recalling the Napoleonic Wars of Liberation. The narrative nevertheless maintains its folk element through simple expression, the prevalence of symbols, such as the rose, the veil and the coin, and the use of oral-culture paradigms, such as the ballad. Indeed, many of the sources identified in the text owe much to the *Volkslied* or ballad as collected by Brentano and Arnim in *Des Knaben Wunderhorn* (1805). This is most notable in relation to the tale of Fair Annie, which is based on the ballad 'Weltlich Recht' ('Worldly Justice'), featured in the collection, which recounts the fate of a mother tried for the unnatural crime of infanticide. There are further grotesque reminders of the *Nachtseite*, in particular the shocking image of the executioner's sword, which moves of its own accord before Annie, and the severed head of the hunter Jürge that bites into the young girl's dress. This use of the supernatural adds to the sense of impending doom, which is skilfully created through a focus on the passing of time as time runs out for Casper, Annie and the old woman. The impression of loss or lack of control is further intensified by both the apron motif, which drags Annie to her final act, and the inner force that drives Casper homewards. This helps create a typically Romantic atmosphere, alien and threatening, which echoes that found in Tieck's text in particular – the self and reason are powerless in the face of such supernatural forces. This late Romantic *Novelle* may point towards the development of future literary trends but it nevertheless distils the essence of the *Kunstmärchen* and clearly demonstrates the established significance of this seminal genre.

CHRONOLOGY

1744 Herder born (d. 1803)

1749 Goethe born (d. 1832)

1759 Schiller born (d. 1805); Sterne, *Tristram Shandy* (completed 1767)

1760 Macpherson, *Ossian* (completed 1765)

1764 Walpole, *The Castle of Otranto*

1765 Percy, *Reliques of Ancient English Poetry*

1767 A. W. Schlegel born (d. 1845)

1772 Novalis born (d. 1801); F. Schlegel born (d. 1829)

1773 Goethe, *Götz von Berlichingen*; Tieck born (d. 1853); Wackenroder born (d. 1798)

1774 Goethe, *The Sorrows of Young Werther*, *Clavigo*

1775 Goethe in Weimar; Sheridan, *The Rivals*

1776 American Declaration of Independence; Hoffmann born (d. 1822); Smith, *Wealth of Nations*

1777 Fouqué born (d. 1843)

1778 Herder, *Folk Ballads* (2 vols., completed 1779); Brentano born (d. 1842)

1781 Kant, *Critique of Pure Reason*; Schiller, *The Robbers*; Arnim born (d. 1831)

1782 Musäus, *German Folk Tales*

1784 Schiller, *Intrigue and Love*; Herder, *Ideas for a Philosophy of the History of Mankind* (completed 1791)

1785 J. Grimm born (d. 1863)

1786 Death of Friedrich the Great; Goethe's Italian journey begins; Wilhelm Grimm born (d. 1859)

1787 Goethe, *Iphigenia in Tauris*; Schiller, *Don Carlos*

1788 Eichendorff born (d. 1857)

1789 French Revolution

1790 Goethe, *Torquato Tasso*

1791 Goethe director of Weimar Theatre

1793 Execution of Louis XVI; beginning of French Revolutionary Wars; Jacobin Terror in France

1794 Beginning of friendship between Goethe and Schiller

1795 Goethe, *Conversations of German Emigrants*; Schiller, *Letters on the Aesthetic Education of Mankind*; Tieck, *William Lovell* (3 vols., completed 1796)

1796 Goethe, *Wilhelm Meister's Apprenticeship*; Lewis, *The Monk*; Napoleon's Italian Campaign

1797 Goethe and Schiller, *Ballads*; Goethe, *Hermann and Dorothea*; Wackenroder and Tieck, *Heartfelt Outpourings of an art-loving Friar*; Tieck, *Folk Tales*; Heine born (died 1856); A. W. Schlegel begins translation of Shakespeare

1798 Tieck, *Franz Sternbald's Wanderings*; Wordsworth, *Lyrical Ballads, The Prelude* (completed 1805)

1799 F. Schlegel, *Lucinde*; Schleiermacher, *Addresses on Religion*; Tieck, *Romantic Literature*; Novalis, *Christendom or Europe* (published 1821)

1800 Schiller, *Maria Stuart*; Novalis, *Hymns to the Night*

1801 Brentano, *Godwi*; F. Schlegel, *Literary Notebooks*

1802 Novalis, *Heinrich von Ofterdingen, The Disciples at Saïs*; Tieck, *The Rune Mountain*

1804 Napoleon crowned emperor; Schiller, *Wilhelm Tell*; Tieck, *Kaiser Octavianus*; Brentano, *Ponce de Leon*

1805 Arnim and Brentano in Heidelberg, begin collecting for *The Boy's Magic Horn* (completed 1808); Scott, *The Lay of the Last Minstrel*

1806 Battle of Jena; end of Holy Roman Empire; defeat of Prussia

1807 Kleist, *Amphitryon*; Hegel, *Phenomenology of the Spirit*; Fichte, *Addresses to the German Nation*; Wordsworth, *Poems*; Byron, *Hours of Idleness*

1808 Goethe, *Faust*, Part I (Part II completed 1832); Kleist, *Penthesilea, The Broken Jug*; Fouqué, *Sigurd the Snake Slayer*

1809 Goethe, *Elective Affinities*; Arnim, *The Winter Garden*; A. W. Schlegel, *Lectures on Dramatic Art and Literature*

1810 Goethe begins *Poetry and Truth*; Scott, *The Lady of the Lake*

1811 Fouqué, *Undine*; Austen, *Sense and Sensibility*

1812 Fouqué, *The Magic Ring*; J. and W. Grimm, *Children's and Household Tales*; Tieck, *Phantasus* (completed 1817); Byron, *Childe Harold's Pilgrimage*, Cantos I and II (III and IV completed 1816 and 1818)

1813 The Battle of Leipzig, Wars of Liberation; Austen, *Pride and Prejudice*

1814 Congress of Vienna; Chamisso, *The Marvellous Tale of Peter Schlemihl*; Hoffmann, *Fantasies*; Scott, *Waverley*

1815 Battle of Waterloo; Brentano, *The Founding of Prague*; Eichendorff, *Premonition and Present*; Hoffmann, *The Devil's Elixirs*, *The Sandman*

1816 Coleridge, *Christabel*

1817 Brentano, *The Tale of Honest Casper and Fair Annie*; Hoffmann, *Nocturnes*

1819 Goethe, *West-eastern Divan*; Hoffmann, *The Brothers Serapion*; Tieck settles in Dresden; Byron, *Don Juan* (completed 1824)

1821 Heine, *Poems*; Scott, *Kenilworth*

TEXTUAL AND
BIBLIOGRAPHICAL NOTE

It is a daunting task to approach texts of the calibre of those chosen for this anthology, particularly when one considers the significance of the individual authors in the context of German literary history. The importance of these texts as historical documents is as potent as their ability to entertain. I have therefore endeavoured, as far as possible, to replicate the tone of the original and avoid any temptation to modernize. Proper names remain as in the original with the exception of the central protagonists of Brentano's tale where the Anglicized version was deemed more suitable. Translations are based on the following editions:

Clemens Brentano, *Gesammelte Schriften*, 9 vols. (Frankfurt am Main: Sauerländer, 1852–5)

Friedrich de la Motte Fouqué, *Ausgewählte Werke*, 12 vols. (Schwetschke: Halle, 1841)

Johann Wolfgang von Goethe, *Sämtliche Werke*, 30 vols. (Stuttgart: Cotta, 1850–51)

Ludwig Tieck, *Schriften*, 12 vols. (Berlin: Reimer, 1828)

Select Bibliography

ROMANTICISM AND THE FAIRY TALE

G. T. Hughes, *German Romantic Literature* (London: Arnold, 1979)

M. Swales, *The German Novelle* (Princeton: Princeton University Press, 1977)

M. Thalmann, *The Romantic Fairy Tale* (Michigan: University of Michigan, 1964)

M. Warner, *From the Beast to the Blonde. On Fairy Tales and their Tellers* (London: Vintage, 1994)

GOETHE

T. J. Reed, *Goethe* (Oxford: OUP, 1984)

J. R. Williams, *The Life of Goethe* (London: Blackwell, 1998)

TIECK

W. J. Lillyman, *Reality's Dark Dream. The Narrative Fiction of Ludwig Tieck* (Berlin and New York: de Gruyter, 1978)

R. Paulin, *Ludwig Tieck. A Literary Biography* (Oxford: OUP, 1985)

FOUQUÉ

W. J. Lillyman, 'Fouqué's *Undine*', *Studies in Romanticism* 10 (1971)

BRENTANO

J. Fetzer, *Clemens Brentano* (Boston: Twayne, 1981)

—*Romantic Orpheus: Profiles of Clemens Brentano* (California, 1974)

The Fairy Tale

JOHANN WOLFGANG VON GOETHE

On the banks of the great river, which was swollen by recent heavy rain, the old ferryman lay fast asleep in his little hut, quite exhausted by the efforts of the day. In the middle of the night, the sound of raised voices roused the old man from his slumbers; they belonged to travellers who wished to be ferried across the raging river.

As he stepped outside, he saw two will-o'-the-wisps hovering above his rowing boat, which was moored near by. They impressed upon him with some urgency that they were in a great hurry and wanted to be taken to the opposite bank immediately. The old man wasted no time; he pushed off and rowed across the river with his customary skill as the strangers whispered to each other rapidly in some foreign tongue. From time to time they would burst into loud laughter, jumping to and fro on the sides and benches, then on the bottom of the boat.

'The boat is rocking!' cried the old man. 'You will make it capsize if you carry on like this; sit down, you will-o'-the-wisps!'

This command caused great hilarity and they made fun of the old man, becoming even more unruly than before. He bore their mischief with patience and soon they landed on the other bank.

'This is for your trouble!' cried the travellers, and, as they shook themselves, a number of glittering gold coins fell into the damp boat.

'For Heaven's sake, what are you doing!' shouted the old man. 'You will bring me bad luck! The river simply detests gold! If a coin were to fall into the water, then it would whip up the most terrible waves and engulf me and my boat in a flash. And who knows what might happen to you; here, keep your money!'

'We cannot take it back; once we have shaken some from our bodies, it is immediately replaced.'

'Then I suppose it is up to me to collect them and bury them ashore,' said the old man as he bent down, placing the coins in his cap.

In the meantime, the will-o'-the-wisps had jumped from the boat.

'Where is my fare?' cried the old man.

'Anyone who will not accept gold must work for nothing!' shouted the will-o'-the-wisps.

'But surely you know that I can only accept fruits of the earth as payment.'

'We spurn them and have never eaten them.'

'But I cannot let you go until you promise to bring me three cabbages, three artichokes and three large onions.'

The will-o'-the-wisps laughed as they made to leave, but found themselves inexplicably rooted to the ground; it was the most unpleasant sensation they had ever experienced. They promised to meet the ferryman's demands immediately, upon which he released them and pushed off from the bank. He was already some distance away when they called after him, 'Old man! Listen. Old man! We forgot the most important thing!' But he was gone and could not hear them. His boat had been carried downstream on the near side of the river to the place where he wanted to bury the dangerous gold, out of reach of the water among some rocks. There he found a deep chasm between two rocks into which he tipped the gold. He then returned to his hut.

The chasm was inhabited by a beautiful green serpent who was roused from her sleep by the ringing sound of the falling coins. The moment she spotted the shining disks she began to gobble them up greedily, carefully seeking out all the coins that had found their way into the bushes and nooks and crannies of the rock.

She had barely finished eating them when she experienced the most delightful sensation as the gold melted inside her, spreading out through her whole body. She noticed with great joy that she had become transparent and begun to glow. She had long been aware that such a wonderful transformation was possible, yet she was unsure just how long her newly acquired brilliance would last. So, driven by curiosity and the burning desire to secure this new gift for the future, she slithered her way out from the cliffs in order to discover who it was that had thrown down the lovely gold. There was no one to be seen. As she slithered along through the undergrowth she was really rather taken with herself and the graceful light that filtered out through the surrounding foliage. The leaves seemed to gleam like emeralds and the flowers were dappled with the hues of many colours. She roamed in vain through the lonely wilderness but her hopes began to rise a little when she came to the plains and saw in the distance a glow that resembled her own. 'Have I found my kin at last?' she cried out as she sped towards the spot. She was untroubled by the difficulties involved in crawling through the marsh and reeds, for although she much preferred to live on dry mountain meadows in high cliff crevices, able to feast on succulent herbs and slake her thirst with tender dew and fresh spring water, she would have done anything demanded of her for the sake of her beloved gold and the promise of the glorious light.

Exhausted, she at last came upon a damp reedy marsh where our two will-o'-the-wisps were at play. She shot forwards to greet them and was delighted to find herself related to such pleasant gentlemen. The flickering lights sidled up to her, leaping to and fro and laughing in their usual manner. 'Dear Aunt,' they said, 'even though you do indeed belong to the horizontal line, it really means nothing; for we are related only through our shared brilliance, for, as you see' (at this point the two flames drew themselves in, discarding their full breadth and making themselves as long and as pointed as possible) 'a slender figure suits us gentlemen of vertical form quite beautifully; do not be offended, my friend, for what family can boast such a thing? Ever since the first will-o'-the-wisp was created, none of our kin has ever had to sit or lie down.'

The serpent felt most uneasy in the company of these relations, for no matter how high she tried to raise her head, she was still forced to lower it to the ground again in order to move, and whereas before she had felt so wonderfully at ease in the dark grove, here her glow seemed to diminish with every moment she spent in the presence of these cousins, so much so that she feared it would eventually extinguish altogether.

Feeling quite embarrassed, she hastily inquired whether the gentlemen could tell her where the glowing gold that had recently fallen into the cliff chasm might have come from; she thought it might have been golden rain that had trickled down from Heaven. The will-o'-the-wisps laughed and shook themselves and a large number of gold coins bounced around them. The serpent went after the coins quickly to eat them up. 'Bon appetit, dear Aunt,' said the charming gentlemen. 'We can offer many more.' They shook themselves a few more times quite vigorously, so much so that the serpent could barely eat the valuable delicacy quickly enough. Her glow became visibly brighter and she shone really quite magnificently. The will-o'-the-wisps, on the other hand, had become quite thin and small, yet without losing anything of their good humour.

'I am forever in your debt,' said the serpent once she had caught her breath again after her meal. 'Ask of me what you will; I will do for you whatever is in my power.'

'Splendid!' cried the will-o'-the-wisps. 'Tell us, where can we find beautiful Lily? Take us as quickly as you can to the palace and gardens of beautiful Lily. We are dying of impatience to throw ourselves at her feet.'

'Such a favour cannot be granted immediately,' replied the serpent with a deep sigh. 'Beautiful Lily dwells on the other side of the river.'

'On the other side of the river! And to think, we have only just come from there this stormy night! How cruel the river is to separate us in this way! Is it not possible to call upon the old man again?'

'It would be in vain,' replied the serpent, 'for even if you were to meet him on this bank, he still would not consent to take you across; he may bring passengers over to this side but he cannot take anyone back to the other.'

'We have got into quite a mess! Is there no other way to cross the water?'

'There are other ways, but not at this moment. I can take you across myself, but not until midday.'

'We do not like to travel at that hour.'

'In that case, you must travel across in the evening on the giant's shadow.'

'How is that done?'

'The great giant, who lives not far from here, can do nothing with his body; his hands are incapable of lifting even a straw, his shoulders would not even bear a bundle of kindling; but his shadow can do a great deal, nay, everything. That is why he is at his most powerful at sunrise and sunset. If you sit in the nape of the shadow's neck as the giant moves towards the river, the shadow will lift you across the water, but this is possible only in the evening. Still, if you make your way, around midday, to the edge of the forest, where the bushes grow close to the water's edge, then I will take you across and introduce you to beautiful Lily; if you fear the midday heat, then you must look for the giant towards evening in yonder cliff-lined bay and he will no doubt oblige.'

The young gentlemen took their leave with a discreet bow. The serpent was pleased to be rid of them, partly in order to enjoy her own brilliance, but also to satisfy a burning curiosity, which had plagued her for some time.

In one particular spot deep among the crevasses where she was wont to slither to and fro, she had made an odd discovery. Despite being forced to make her way through these dark abysses without the benefit of light, she was able to identify quite accurately many objects just by touching them, with any irregular forms encountered usually being those fashioned by Nature; one minute she was sliding in between the jagged points of gigantic crystals, the next she was brushing over the rough surface of a seam of pure silver. One precious stone after another saw the light of day as she laboured to bring them to the surface. Yet, in one enclosed chasm, she had, much to her surprise, felt objects that betrayed the creative hand of man. Smooth walls, which she could not ascend, sharp, regular edges, well-formed columns and, strangest of all, human figures around which she slithered repeatedly and which she guessed to be of ore or highly polished marble. She now hoped finally to bring all these sensations together through the sense of sight and to confirm what she had until now only suspected. She now believed herself capable of illuminating this wonderful underground vault with her own light and hoped to become fully acquainted with these strange objects at once. She hurried on, following the customary path, and soon found the crevice through which she usually slipped.

Once there, she looked around, filled with curiosity. Although her glow was unable to illuminate all the objects in the cavern at once, those nearest to her became clear enough. She found herself gazing with wonder and reverence at a bejewelled recess, which housed the statue of a venerable king made of pure gold. The statue was taller than a man in size, yet the figure was more that of a small than a large man. His well-formed body was covered with a simple cloak and a garland of oak leaves encircled his head.

No sooner had the serpent beheld this vision than the king began to speak and asked, 'Where have you come from?'

'From the chasms where the gold dwells,' replied the serpent.

'What is more magnificent than gold?' asked the king.

'Light,' replied the serpent.

'What is more pleasant than light?' asked the former.

'Conversation,' replied the latter.

During their conversation, the serpent glanced sideways and caught sight of another magnificent image in the next recess, that of a silver king whose figure was long and rather slight. His body was adorned with an elaborate cloak and his crown, belt and sceptre were all bedecked with precious jewels. There was a cheerful pride about his appearance and he seemed about to speak when a dark vein, which ran through the marble wall, suddenly became illuminated, filling the entire temple with a pleasant glow. The light enabled the serpent to see the third king, whose powerful figure was made of ore. He sat there, leaning on a club, adorned with a laurel wreath, and had more the appearance of a rock than a man. She was about to turn round to look at the fourth king, who stood some distance away from her, when the wall opened up, causing the illuminated vein to flash like a bolt of lightning and disappear.

A man of medium stature emerged and beckoned to the serpent. He was dressed as a peasant and in his hand carried a small lamp whose steady flame was a pleasure to behold and which lit up the whole cathedral in a wonderful fashion, yet without casting any shadow whatsoever.

'Why have you come when we already have light?' asked the golden king.

'You know that I may not illuminate darkness.'

'Will my kingdom come to an end?' asked the silver king.

'It may be late or never,' replied the old man.

The iron king spoke in a thundering voice. 'When shall I arise?'

'Soon,' replied the old man.

'With whom am I to unite?' asked the king.

'With your older brother,' said the old man.

'What will become of the youngest?' asked the king.

'He will rest,' said the old man.

'I am not tired!' cried the fourth king in a rough, faltering voice.

While they were speaking, the serpent had slithered quietly around the temple, surveying everything as she went, and was now examining the fourth king at close quarters. He stood leaning against a pillar, his imposing figure more melancholy than handsome. It was difficult to discern the metal from which he had been cast. Looking closely, it was a mixture of the three metals from which his brothers had been made but they had not been cast well together; gold and silver veins ran irregularly through an iron mass and gave the image an unpleasant appearance.

Meanwhile, the golden king asked the old man, 'How many secrets do you know?'

'Three,' replied the old man.

'Which is the most important?' asked the silver king.

'The most obvious,' replied the old man.

'Will you reveal it to us?' asked the iron king.

'As soon as I know the fourth,' said the old man.

'What does it matter to me!' the alloy king mumbled to himself.

'I know the fourth secret,' said the serpent as she approached the old man and hissed something in his ear.

'The time is come!' cried the old man in a tremendous voice. The temple echoed, the metal statues rang and, in the same instant, the old man vanished to the west, the serpent to the east, each passing straight through the chasms in the rocks with incredible speed.

As the old man hurried through the passageways they immediately filled with gold in his wake, for his lamp had the amazing ability to turn all stone to gold, all wood to silver, dead animals to precious stones and all metal to dust; to achieve this impact, however, it must illuminate alone. If another light were near it, then it would seem to give little more than a pleasant glow whose light refreshed all living things.

The old man entered his hut, which was built on the side of the mountain, and found his wife in great anguish. She sat by the fire and wept and could not be consoled. 'How unhappy I am!' she cried out. 'I did not want to let you go out today!'

'What is wrong?' asked the old man calmly.

'No sooner had you gone,' she sobbed, 'than two unruly travellers appeared at the door; I unwisely let them in, they seemed well-mannered, decent people; they were clad in light flames, one might have thought they were will-o'-the-wisps; no sooner were they in the house than they began to flatter me in a quite inappropriate manner and became so importunate that I am quite ashamed to think of it.'

'Now, now,' replied the old man, 'the gentlemen were most likely only joking; for given your age they ought to have been satisfied with ordinary politeness.'

'What do you mean, given my age!' cried the woman. 'Am I ever to be reminded of my age? How old am I then? Ordinary politeness indeed! I know what I know. Just look around you, how the walls look; just look at the old stones I haven't seen for a hundred years; they licked off all the gold, you can't imagine with what skill, and all the time assuring me it tasted better than common gold. And once they had cleared the walls they seemed in the best of moods and, indeed, were soon much larger and broader and shone more. But then they started their devilment again, caressing me again, calling me their queen; then they shook themselves and a load of gold coins fell around them; you can see them still glinting under the bench; but what a stroke of bad luck! Our little pug ate a few of them and look, there he is by the fireplace, dead, the poor animal! I am inconsolable. I noticed it only after they had gone, otherwise I would never have promised to pay their debt to the ferryman.'

'What do they owe?' asked the old man.

'Three cabbages, three artichokes and three onions,' said the old woman. 'I have promised to take them to the river as soon as it is daylight.'

'You can do them the favour,' said the old man, 'for they will soon repay us the service.'

'Whether they will truly be of service to us, I cannot tell, but they swore to do so.'

Meanwhile, the fire in the grate had burnt itself out. The old man covered the coals with a pile of ash and swept the glinting gold coins to one side. Now his lamp was once more the sole source of light. As the beautiful glow spread, the walls were covered in gold and the pug was turned into the most beautiful onyx imaginable. The mixture of brown and black in the precious stone made him into quite the rarest work of art.

'Take your basket,' said the old man, 'and place the onyx in it; then take the three cabbages, the three artichokes and the three onions, place them round it and take them to the river. Have the serpent take you across at midday and pay a visit to beautiful Lily. Take the onyx to her; her touch will bring him back to life, just as it usually kills all living things; she shall have in him a loyal companion. Tell her not to be sad, for she will soon be delivered; tell her to consider a great misfortune as her greatest blessing, for the time is come.'

The old woman packed her basket and set off at the break of day. The rising sun shone brightly above the river, which shimmered in the distance; the woman walked slowly, for the basket weighed heavily on her head, not, however, because of the onyx, for any dead things she carried were weightless and would cause the basket to rise into the air and float above her head; yet a fresh vegetable or a living creature were extremely heavy for her. She struggled along for some time before something startled her, causing her to stop suddenly in her tracks; she had almost trodden on the giant's shadow, which was coming towards her across the plain. Just then, she caught sight of the monstrous giant as he emerged from the water after bathing. She was unsure how to avoid him. As soon as he noticed her, he greeted her jovially as the hands of his shadow grabbed at her basket. With ease and dexterity the shadow stole a cabbage, an artichoke and an onion from the basket and placed them in the mouth of the giant, who then carried on upstream and left the woman where she stood.

She wondered whether it might not be better to turn back in order to replace the missing pieces from her vegetable garden. Yet, she carried on and was still deliberating when she reached the river bank. She sat for a long time awaiting the ferryman. She eventually spied him bringing a mysterious traveller with him across the river. A handsome young man of noble appearance disembarked from the rowing boat.

'What have you there?' asked the old man.

'The vegetables owed to you by the will-o'-the-wisps,' replied the old woman and pointed to her wares. When the old man saw there were only two of each he became angry and assured her he could not take them. The woman pleaded with him insistently, telling him that she could not return home now for her burden was heavy and the journey long. He remained resolute in his refusal, assuring her that it did not depend on him.

'Whatever is owed to me must be kept together for nine hours and I may not take anything for myself until I have handed a third of it over to the river.'

After much discussion the old man finally conceded that there was another way. 'If you make a pledge to the river yourself and acknowledge yourself as debtor then I shall take the six pieces, but there is some danger involved.'

'If I keep my word, surely there is no danger?'

'None at all. Put your hand in the river,' continued the old man, 'and promise that you will settle the debt within twenty-four hours.'

The old woman did as he said but what a fright she had when she saw her hand emerge from the water as black as coal. She scolded the old man bitterly, assuring him that her hands had always been her best feature and that she had always managed to keep them white and delicate despite all the hard work she had to do. She looked at her hand with alarm and cried out in desperation, 'Oh, no! Even worse! Look, it has shrunk, it is much smaller than the other!'

'It only seems that way now,' said the old man. 'If you do not keep your word, it might become reality. The hand will shrink and shrink gradually and then finally disappear altogether, yet you shall not lose the use of it. It will function as before, only no one will be able to see it.'

'I would rather not have the use of it at all and keep my misfortune a secret,' said the old woman. 'Still, this is all of no matter for I shall keep my word and be rid of this black skin and this worry soon.' She hurriedly took the basket, which raised itself above her head and floated freely in the air, and hastened after the young man who was making his way slowly along the river bank, obviously deep in thought. His noble figure and his strange attire had made quite an impression upon her.

His breast was adorned with glittering armour through which all the movements of his corpulent frame could be seen. A crimson robe hung round his shoulders, his bare head was a mass of beautiful brown curls; his handsome face was exposed to the rays of the sun, as were his elegant feet. He wandered barefoot, crossing the hot sand with ease. Yet, some inner pain seemed to deaden all outward expression.

The garrulous old woman tried to engage him in conversation but he barely responded. Eventually, despite his enchanting and beautiful eyes, she grew weary of her vain efforts to engage him in conversation and took her leave, 'You are walking too slowly for me, sir, I dare not waste a single moment if I am to cross to the other side on the green serpent and bring beautiful Lily this splendid present from my husband.' With these words, she set off in haste. But then, just as hastily, the handsome young man gathered himself and hurried after her.

'You are on your way to beautiful Lily!' he cried. 'Then we are heading the same way. What kind of present is it that you are taking?'

'Sir,' replied the woman, 'it is hardly fitting, having evaded my questions so churlishly before, to inquire with such enthusiasm after my secrets. However, if you are prepared to enter into a bargain with me and tell me your tale, then I shall not remain secretive about myself and my present for long.' They were soon in agreement; the woman told him of her circumstances and all about the dog and allowed him to see the wonderful present.

He immediately lifted the precious figure from the basket and held the pug, who appeared to be asleep, in his arms. 'Fortunate animal!' he cried. 'You will feel the touch of her hands, you will be brought back to life by her, unlike the living who flee from her touch so that they might escape a terrible fate. Yet, what do I mean – a terrible fate! Is it not far more awful and more frightening to be paralysed by her presence than it would be to die at her hands! Look at me!' he said to the old woman. 'What miserable circumstances I have had to endure in my life. This armour, which has seen me through wars with honour, this cloak, which I have earned by wise government, have been soured by Fate, the former now a needless burden, the latter but a meaningless ornament. Crown, sceptre and sword are gone; I am as naked and destitute as every other son of the earth, for such is the spell of her beautiful blue eyes that they draw the strength from every living thing and those not killed by the touch of her hand find themselves reduced to mere breathing shadows.'

He continued to lament his fate, not satisfying in any measure the curiosity of the old woman, who was less interested in his mental than his physical circumstances. She could gather neither the name of his father nor his kingdom. He stroked the stony little pug, which, now warmed by the sun and the young man's embrace, seemed almost alive. He asked many questions about the man with the lamp, about the effects of the sacred light and seemed to see in these the promise of relief from his miserable condition.

As they continued their conversation, in the distance they caught sight of the majestic arc of the bridge, glistening wondrously in the sunshine as it spanned the river from one bank to the other. Both were astounded, for they had never before seen it look so magnificent.

'How can it be!' cried the prince. 'Was it not already quite beautiful enough when it stood before us as if made from jasper and opal? Dare we even set foot on it now, for it seems to be made of emeralds and all manner of chrysolite!' Neither knew anything of the changes that the serpent had undergone: for, indeed, it was the serpent who spanned the river each midday and who now stood before them in the form of a quite splendid bridge. The travellers stepped upon it with reverence and crossed in silence.

Scarcely had they reached the opposite bank than the bridge began to swing and move, gradually sinking down towards the surface of the water. The green serpent assumed her normal shape and glided after the travellers on to dry land. The pair had only just uttered their thanks to the serpent for allowing them to cross on her back when they became aware that there must be others present who were nevertheless invisible to them. They heard a hissing sound next to them to which the serpent responded in kind; they paid close attention and were eventually able to make out something of the conversation. Two alternating voices could be heard:

'We must first of all make a secret visit to the gardens of beautiful Lily to see what we can see. Then, as soon as night falls and we are relatively presentable, we request that you introduce us to the perfect beauty. You shall find us on the shore of the great lake.'

'As you wish,' replied the serpent, and her hissing voice vanished in the air.

Our three travellers then discussed in which order they should appear before the beautiful one, for although many people could be in her presence at one time, they must come and go individually in order to avoid terrible suffering.

The old woman approached the garden first, carrying the transformed dog in her basket, and sought an audience with her benefactress. The latter was easily found for she sang at her harp; the melodious tones appeared first as ripples on the surface of the lake, then as a light breeze, rustling the grass and the bushes. She sat in a secluded bower in the shade of a group of trees and the very sight of her filled the eyes, ears and heart of the old woman with renewed delight. As she approached her, the old woman was convinced that the beautiful one had grown even more beautiful in her absence and, while still some distance away, she greeted the charming young girl with words of praise.

'Oh, what a joy it is to behold you! How heavenly your presence is! How delightfully the harp rests in your lap; how softly your arms embrace it; how it seems to long to be laid on your breast and how tender it sounds at the touch of your slender fingers! Thrice happy the youth who might replace it!'

As she spoke, she came closer; beautiful Lily opened her eyes, let her hands fall and replied, 'Do not sadden me with untimely praise; it only makes my misfortune seem worse. Look, here at my feet lies the poor canary who always used to accompany my songs so merrily; he was in the habit of sitting on my harp, carefully positioned so that I might avoid touching him; this morning, refreshed by sleep, I began to sing a peaceful melody; my little songster sang as beautifully as he had ever done when suddenly a hawk darted over my head; the poor little animal flew to my bosom in fright and I instantly felt the last gasp of a departing life. It is certainly true that one glance from me sent the villain plummeting helplessly towards the water, but what good is my punishment; my dearest one is dead and his grave will number but another of the melancholy bushes that fill my garden.'

'Come now, beautiful Lily!' cried the woman as she dried her own tears, which had fallen as she listened to the girl's sad tale. 'Gather yourself; my husband bids me to tell you to temper your grief and to see such great misfortune as a harbinger of the greatest happiness; for the time has come; but really, this world is a strange old place,' continued the old woman. 'Look at my hand, how black it has become! Truly, it has become much smaller, I must hurry before it vanishes altogether! Why did I make such a rash promise to the will-o'-the-wisps; why did I have to meet with the giant; and why did I have to dip my hand into the river? Can you oblige me with a cabbage, an artichoke and an onion? Then I can take them to the river and my hand will be white once more so that I might almost compare its fairness to yours.'

'You might at best find cabbages and onions, but you would look for artichokes in vain, I fear. None of the plants in my garden bear flowers or fruit; yet every dry twig that I break off and plant on the grave of a loved one grows high into the air. And I must watch them flourish, all these clusters of trees, these copses and groves. These lofty pines, these towering cypresses, each great oak and beech, all were once mere paltry twigs, planted by my own hand in otherwise barren earth, each a sad monument to a lost companion.'

The old woman paid little attention to this speech, gazing instead at her hand that, in the presence of beautiful Lily, seemed to darken and shrink yet more with each passing moment. She was about to gather up her basket and rush off, when she remembered that she had forgotten the most important thing. She took the transformed dog and sat it down on the grass, a little away from the beautiful one. 'My husband sends you this token,' she said. 'You know that your touch can bring this precious stone to life. This good and loyal animal will bring you much joy, and my sadness at losing him will surely be lessened by the knowledge that he is now yours.'

Beautiful Lily looked at the animal with pleasure and, it seemed, amazement.

'Many things now combine to bring me great hope,' she said. 'But, alas, is it not our nature to wrongly foresee happiness in the midst of great misfortune?

> 'What good to me are many omens fair?
> A sweet bird killed, a friend in black dismay.
> This small dog now a jewel beyond compare.
> Was he sent by the lamp to guide the way?
>
> 'Kept hidden far away from the life I adore,
> Tears and misery, the only friends I know.
> Tell me why no temple stands on the shore?
> Tell me why no bridge spans the waters below?'

The good old woman had waited impatiently as beautiful Lily sang this song to the tuneful accompaniment of her harp and, indeed, it would have delighted anyone else who happened to hear it. She was just about to take her leave when the arrival of the green serpent delayed her once more. The latter had heard the final lines of the song and sought to comfort beautiful Lily with bold words of encouragement.

'The prophecy of the bridge has been fulfilled!' she cried. 'Just ask this good woman how magnificent the arch looks now. What was once mere jasper, too opaque to let the light shine through except at its very edges, is now formed of the most beautiful transparent precious stone. No beryl has ever been so bright, no emerald so magnificent.'

'I wish you luck with it,' said Lily, 'but forgive me if I do not believe you when you say that the prophecy has been truly fulfilled. Only those on foot may cross your lofty arch, yet it was promised to us that horses and coaches and travellers of every sort would be able to wander together freely to and fro across the bridge. Did the prophecy not speak of great pillars that would rise from the waters themselves?'

The old woman, who was still staring intently at her hand, interrupted the conversation at this point and bid them farewell. 'Stay a moment longer,' said beautiful Lily, 'and take my poor canary with you. Ask the lamp to turn him into a beautiful topaz so that my touch might bring him back to life and he and your dear pug shall be my favourite distractions; but hurry all you can for when the sun begins to set a vile decay will seize the poor creature and destroy his beautiful form for ever.'

The old woman carefully wrapped the tiny corpse in some soft leaves, placed it in her basket and hurried away.

'Anyway, despite what you might think, the temple has been built,' said the serpent, continuing their conversation.

'If so, then it does not yet stand on the river bank,' replied the beautiful one.

'It still lies in the depths of the earth,' said the serpent. 'I have seen the kings and spoken with them.'

'And when shall they rise?' asked Lily.

'I heard a great voice thunder round the temple walls,' replied the serpent: ' "The time has come!" '

A joyful expression spread across the face of beautiful Lily. 'That is the second time today that I have heard these happy words spoken,' she said. 'When will the day dawn when I hear them three times?'

She rose to her feet. A charming young girl sprang instantly from the bushes and gathered up her harp. She was followed by another who lifted the carved ivory stool upon which the beautiful one had been sitting, folded it up and placed the silver cushion under her arm.

Then a third appeared, carrying a huge parasol embroidered with pearls, and waited to see whether Lily wished to go for a walk. These girls were beautiful beyond description but yet their beauty was surpassed by Lily's and each had to agree their charms could not compare with those of their mistress.

Meanwhile beautiful Lily had been examining the wonderful pug with a look of pleasure. She bent down to touch him and he leapt to his feet in a flash. He looked around brightly and began running to and fro until he finally rushed to greet his benefactress with friendly enthusiasm. She picked him up and held him close to her bosom. 'It matters not to me that you are cold and only half alive,' she cried, 'your companionship is still most welcome to me; I will love you dearly, tease you playfully, caress you tenderly and hold you dear to my heart.' With that, she let him run off a little way, only to call him back and then chase him off again. She teased and played with him in the grass with such joy and innocence, that, at that moment, it was impossible not to share her delight, just as earlier every heart had shared her sorrow.

This merriment was interrupted by the arrival of the melancholy young man. He entered looking much as we have already described him, only now the heat of the day seemed to have wearied him even more and, indeed, he grew paler with every passing moment in the presence of his beloved. On his wrist he carried the hawk, which sat as peacefully as a dove with his wings drooping down.

'I do not find it fitting that you bring before me the hateful animal, nay, monster, that this very day caused the death of my dear little songster!' shouted Lily.

'Do not blame the unhappy bird!' replied the youth. 'Far rather blame yourself and your fate; and then let me join him in shared misery.'

In the meantime the pug kept seeking the attention of the beautiful one who rewarded her precious favourite with open affection. She clapped her hands to chase him away; then she ran to bring him back. She tried to catch him as he fled and chased him away when he tried to press against her. The youth watched in silence and with growing annoyance; eventually, as she lifted up the horrible animal, which he found quite repulsive, hugged it to her white breast and kissed its black nose with her heavenly lips, he lost all patience and cried out in sheer desperation:

'Must I, forced by Fate to live in your presence and yet doomed for ever to be parted from you; must I, bereft of everything, even my own self, because of you; must I be subjected to the sight of such an unnatural monstrosity being allowed to bring you joy, hold your attention and enjoy your embrace! Am I to continue to wander to and fro, to mark out over and over the miserable circle as I journey across the river and back again? No, there is still a flicker of the old fire in my breast; let it muster a final flourish now! If mere stones may repose upon your bosom then let me be turned to stone; if your touch can kill, then let me die at your hands.'

With these words he made a violent movement towards the beautiful one; the hawk flew from his hand as he rushed towards her; she held out her hands to keep him away and touched him all the sooner. His senses left him and with horror she felt the weight of the beautiful burden as it sank on her breast. She stepped back with a cry and the handsome youth sank, lifeless, from her arms and slid to the ground.

The deed was done! Dear, sweet Lily stood motionless, staring in horror at the lifeless corpse. Her heart stood still, her eyes shed no tears. The pug tried in vain to elicit a friendly response from her; it seemed as if the world had come to an end with the death of her friend yet she sought no help in her silent despair for there was none to be had.

The serpent responded in quite the opposite fashion, seeming all the more eager to help; her thoughts seemed to be of salvation and, indeed, her strange movements managed to at least temporarily postpone the immediate consequences of this terrible misfortune. She encompassed the corpse in a wide circle with her lithe body, held the end of her tail in her mouth and lay quite still.

Shortly afterwards, one of the charming maidens approached the beautiful one with the ivory stool and bade her mistress be seated; then came the second one with a fire-coloured veil with which she used to adorn rather than cover Lily's head; the third handed her the harp and no sooner had Lily clasped the splendid instrument and played a few notes on the strings than the first maid returned with a lustrous oval mirror and held it in front of the beautiful one, capturing her fair countenance and reflecting the most pleasant features Nature could ever hope to create. Sorrow increased her beauty, the veil heightened her charm, the harp added to her grace, and no matter how much one might wish to see her sad situation altered, one could not help but hope that this vision might last for ever.

Gazing silently at the mirror, she began to play. Her pain seemed to intensify and the strings responded with passion to her misery; a few times she opened her mouth to sing but found herself unable; then her pain turned to tears. Two of the maidens went to lend her their support as the harp fell into her lap to be caught up and laid aside by a third watchful servant. 'Who shall fetch the man with the lamp before nightfall?' asked the serpent in a low, barely audible hiss. The maidens looked at each other and Lily's tears rolled faster down her cheeks.

At that moment the woman with the basket returned quite out of breath. 'I am lost! I am crippled!' she cried out. 'Look how my hand has almost vanished; neither the ferryman nor the giant would take me across because I was still in debt to the river; I offered a hundred cabbages and a hundred onions, but all in vain; no one wants more than the three pieces and there is not an artichoke to be found for miles around.'

'Forget your distress,' said the serpent, 'and try to help here; who knows, it might solve your problem too. Hurry all you can to find the will-o'-the-wisps: it is still too light to see them but you might hear them laughing and fluttering about. If they hurry then the giant will take them across the river and they can seek out the man with the lamp and send him to us.'

The woman hurried as fast as she could and the serpent seemed as impatient as was Lily for the two of them to return. Unfortunately, the sun's rays now shone their golden light on only the very highest tree-tops of the forest and long shadows were cast over lake and meadow; the serpent fidgeted impatiently and Lily's tears continued to flow.

In this moment of anguish, the serpent looked anxiously around for she feared the sun would set at any moment, allowing vile decay to break through the magic circle and fall inexorably upon the youth. At last, high in the air, she saw the hawk's crimson breast feathers gleaming in the last rays of the sun. She shook herself for joy at the sight of this good omen and, indeed, she was not to be disappointed for shortly afterwards the man with the lamp came into view gliding over the lake as if he were skating.

The serpent stayed where she was as Lily stood up and called to him, 'What good spirit has sent you at the very moment when we longed for and needed you most?'

'The spirit of my lamp drove me onwards and the hawk showed me the way,' replied the old man. 'The lamp flickers whenever I am needed and I need only look around in the Heavens for a sign until a bird or a meteor shows me the direction in which I am to go. Be calm, dear beautiful child! I do not know whether I can help; sometimes it requires the timely union of many rather than the efforts of one individual to put things right. We must wait and hope.' Turning to the serpent, he said, 'Keep your circle closed.' He sat down next to her on a mound of earth, held his lamp above the corpse and said, 'Bring the dear canary too and lay him in the circle!' The maids lifted the tiny corpse from the basket, which the old woman had left behind, and did as he asked.

Meanwhile, the sun had set and, as darkness fell, the serpent and the lamp began to give off their customary glow. They were joined by Lily's veil, which glowed softly and lit up her pale cheeks and white complexion as gently as the early morning sun. Now and again they would look at one another in silent contemplation, their fear and sadness tempered by the promise of happiness.

Everyone was delighted to see the old woman arrive in the company of the two-will-o'-the-wisps. The pair must have dallied a fair deal in the meantime for they were once again extremely thin but consequently all the more well-behaved in the presence of the princess and the other ladies, with whom they began to converse on quite mundane matters with the greatest of confidence and a witty turn of phrase. They were particularly taken by the veil that endowed Lily and her companions with such an aura of charm. The ladies cast their eyes down in modesty;

the flattery seemed to heighten their beauty even more. Everyone was happy and contented except for the old woman. Despite the assurances of her husband that her hand could become no smaller as long as it remained illuminated by his lamp, she repeatedly lamented that if things continued as they were, then, before midnight struck, her noble limb would surely have disappeared altogether.

The old man with the lamp had been listening intently to the conversation of the will-o'-the-wisps and was particularly pleased to see Lily amused and distracted by their chattering. Indeed, the midnight hour had come without anyone noticing. The old man looked up to the stars and began to speak: 'We have come together at this happy hour, now each must fulfil their role, each must do their duty, for then universal happiness will dissolve all individual pain, just as universal misfortune destroys individual joy.'

No sooner had he spoken these words than the air was filled with a strange murmuring as each of those present gave voice to the task that they must complete. Only the three maidens remained silent; one had fallen asleep by the harp, the other by the parasol and the third next to the chair, and one could not blame them for it was late. The will-o'-the-wisps, having at first paid some polite attention to the maidens, had then devoted themselves solely to Lily for she was the most beautiful by far.

The old man turned to the hawk and said, 'Hold up the mirror and let the reflection of the sun's first rays illuminate their sleeping faces as it shines down from on high so that they might come awake once more.'

Then the serpent began to move, uncoiling her circle and slowly winding her way towards the river. The two will-o'-the-wisps followed her with such solemnity that one might have thought them quite serious in character. The old woman and her husband took hold of the basket whose soft glow had gone unnoticed until now; they stretched it from both sides and it grew larger and began to glow even more. Then they placed the young man's lifeless body into it and laid the canary on his breast. The basket rose in the air, floating above the old woman's head as she followed on behind the will-o'-the-wisps. Beautiful Lily lifted the pug in her arms and followed the old woman.

The man with the lamp joined the procession at the rear as the countryside around them was bathed in the fantastic glow of the many lights.

Upon reaching the river, they were more than a little surprised to find a magnificent arch spanning the water below; it was, of course, the goodly serpent who had gone on ahead to prepare this glimmering path for them. The translucent shimmer of the precious stone was as beautiful by night as it had been by day. The clear arch cut high into the dark sky, while underneath rays of light shot towards the centre, highlighting the pliable strength of the structure. As the procession slowly made its way across, the ferryman looked on in wonder from afar, watching the glowing arch from his little hut as the strange lights moved across it. They had scarcely set foot on the other side when the arch began to sway as it sank down to the surface of the water, echoing the movement of the waves. The serpent soon joined them on the shore and reformed her circle around the basket, which had once more lowered itself to the ground. The old man bent down towards her and asked, 'What is your decision?'

'To sacrifice myself before I am sacrificed by others,' replied the serpent. 'Promise me that you will leave no stone on dry land.'

The old man gave her his word and then turned to Lily. 'Touch the snake with your left hand and your beloved with the right.' Then Lily knelt down and touched both serpent and corpse. Almost immediately, the latter seemed to come to life. He began to stir in the basket, then raised himself and sat upright; Lily wanted to embrace him there and then but the old man held her back. Instead, he helped the youth to his feet and guided him as he stepped out of the basket and moved away from the circle.

The young man stood up straight, the canary fluttered on his shoulder; both were alive again although their faculties were yet to be restored. The handsome youth's eyes were open but he could not see or, rather, he seemed to view everything with an air of indifference. The others had only just begun to accustom themselves to this miracle when they began to notice an odd change at work in the serpent. Her beautiful slender body had dispersed into thousands and thousands of glittering precious stones. In rushing to make a grab for her basket, the old woman had collided with her clumsily and there was nothing more to be seen of the serpent's former shape except for a circle of beautiful glittering jewels lying in the grass.

The old man immediately made to gather up the stones and put them in the basket with the help of his wife. Together they carried the basket to a special place on the river where the old man thrust the entire load into the water, much to the dismay of beautiful Lily and his wife, who would have liked some of it for themselves. The jewels gleamed beneath the waves like brilliant stars and it was impossible to tell whether they had disappeared into the distance or simply sunk to the bottom.

The old man then addressed the will-o'-the-wisps respectfully. 'Gentlemen,' he said, 'I shall now show you the way and clear the path so that you might do us the kind service of opening the door to the shrine through which we must enter. No one can unlock it but you.'

The will-o'-the-wisps bowed in accordance and joined the procession at the rear. The old man took his lamp and went towards the rocky cliffs, which parted before him. The young man followed, his movements still quite mechanical as Lily lingered, silent and unsure, some distance behind him. The old woman did not wish to be left behind and stretched out her hand so that the light of her husband's lamp might illuminate it. Finally the will-o'-the-wisps brought up the rear, bowing the tops of their flames together as they spoke.

They had not gone far when the procession found itself before a huge iron gateway whose doors were held shut by a golden lock. The old man called straight away for the will-o'-the-wisps, who needed little encouragement as they greedily consumed the lock and bolt with their most pointed flames.

The iron resounded loudly as the doors sprang open and soon the venerable figures of the four kings came into view, illuminated by the flickering lights as the procession entered the shrine. They all bowed before the honourable rulers, particularly the will-o'-the-wisps, who bowed lowest of all.

After a pause, the golden king asked, 'Where have you come from?'

'From the world,' answered the old man.

'Where are you going?' asked the silver king.

'Back out into the world,' said the old man.

'What do you want with us?' asked the iron king.

'To accompany you,' said the old man.

The alloy king was about to speak when the golden king turned to the will-o'-the-wisps, who had come up quite close to his side. 'Get away from me, my gold is not for you.'

Then they turned to the silver king and sidled up to him, his apparel gleaming quite beautifully as it reflected their yellow glow. 'You are most welcome,' he said, 'but I cannot feed you; satisfy yourselves elsewhere and then bring me your light.'

They moved away and stole past the iron king, who seemed not to notice them, towards the alloy king. 'Who shall rule the world?' he asked in a stammering voice.

'Whosoever stands upright,' replied the old man.

'That is me!' said the alloy king.

'All will be revealed,' said the old man, 'for the time has come.'

Beautiful Lily embraced the old man and kissed him with great affection. 'Dear father,' she said, 'I thank you a thousand times for now I have heard these prophetic words three times.'

She had barely finished speaking when she was forced to cling even more tightly to the old man, for the earth beneath them began to tremble. The old woman and the youth held on to each other; only the fluttering will-o'-the-wisps remained unperturbed.

The whole temple seemed to move like a ship easing itself out of port with its anchor raised. The depths of the earth seemed to open up before it as it carved its way through, yet there was no impact and no rock stood in its path.

For a few moments it was as if a fine rain had begun to drizzle through the opening in the dome. The old man held Lily tighter and said, 'We are under the river and have almost reached our goal.'

Shortly afterwards they thought they had come to a halt but they were mistaken; the temple was now moving upwards. There was a strange roaring sound above their heads. A confusion of beams and rafters began to crash through the opening in the dome. Lily and the old woman leapt aside. The man with the lamp seized hold of the young man and stayed where he was. The ferryman's little hut, which had been torn from the ground and consumed by the temple as it rose upwards, now sank gradually to the floor, burying the youth and the old man beneath it.

The women screamed out loud as the temple shuddered to a halt like a ship that had unexpectedly run aground. They circled anxiously round the hut in the darkness. The doors were locked and there was no response to their knocking. They knocked louder and were rather surprised when, eventually, the wood began to make a ringing sound. The power of the lamp locked inside the hut had turned it to silver from the inside out. It was not long before even its form began to change as the precious metal abandoned the lowly form of boards, rafters and beams and transformed itself into a magnificent structure of the most elaborate design. A quite beautiful little temple – or, at the very least, an altar most deserving of its place there – now stood in the centre of the great edifice.

The young man began climbing upwards by means of an inner staircase as the man with the lamp lit the way. Another figure, dressed in a short white tunic with a silver rudder in his hand, could be seen assisting the youth. He was immediately recognizable as the ferryman, the former occupant of the transformed hut.

Beautiful Lily climbed the outer stair, which led from the temple up to the altar, but she was still forced to remain at a distance from her beloved. The old woman, whose hand continued to grow smaller in the absence of the lamp, cried out, 'Am I still doomed to be unhappy? In the midst of so many miracles, is there no miracle that will save my hand?'

Her husband pointed to the open doorway and said, 'Look, day is breaking, hurry and bathe in the river.'

'What manner of advice is that!' she cried. 'Am I to become black all over and disappear completely? I have not yet settled my debt.'

'Just go and do as I say,' said the old man. 'All debts are now cancelled.'

The old woman sped away and at that moment the rays of the rising sun shone upon the great dome. The old man stepped between the youth and the maiden and cried in a loud voice: 'There are three things that rule this earth: wisdom, light and power.' At the mention of the first of these, the golden king stood up; at the second, the silver; and, at the mention of the third, the iron king slowly raised himself up as the alloy king sat down awkwardly.

Whoever saw him could not help but laugh, despite his solemn appearance, for he was neither seated nor lying down, nor was he even propped up against anything, but had instead slumped down in a most ungainly manner.

The will-o'-the-wisps, having busied themselves with him for quite some time, now stepped aside. Despite appearing rather pale in the morning light, they looked once more well-fed and in full flame, for they had skilfully licked out all the golden veins from the colossal figure with their pointed tongues. The irregular cavities that this action had caused had remained open for a while, allowing the figure to maintain his original form. However, once even the very finest veins had been consumed, the figure began to collapse and, unfortunately, at precisely those points that normally remain unaltered when a figure is seated; in contrast, the joints that should have been able to bend remained quite stiff. Those unable to laugh were forced to turn away; the object, neither form nor ruin, was hideous to see.

The man with the lamp led the handsome youth, who still maintained his rather vacant appearance, down from the altar and towards the iron king. There, at the feet of the powerful nobleman, lay a sword in an iron sheath. The youth took it and fastened it to his belt.

'The sword to the left, the right side free!' the great monarch cried.

They then approached the silver king who offered the young man his sceptre. The latter took it with his left hand as the king spoke to him softly, 'Take good care of the flock!'

As they neared him, the golden king laid the garland of oak leaves upon the youth's head, an expression of fatherly affection upon his aged face, and said, 'Always honour the highest!'

The old man had been observing the youth very carefully as these dealings took place. With the sword secured to his side, the latter's chest began to heave, his arms moved more freely and his feet trod more firmly. The touch of the sceptre seemed to temper his strength, but, at the same time, that very strength was reinforced, this time endowed with a certain, indescribable grace. Yet, it was only once the oak garland had settled upon his curls that his features began to awaken. His eyes gleamed with indescribable passion. The first word to pass his lips was 'Lily'.

'Dearest Lily!' he exclaimed as he rushed up the silver staircase towards her, to where she had observed his progress from the altar balustrade. 'Dearest Lily, what more can a man wish for than the innocence and the sweet affection that your love brings to me! Oh, my friend,' he continued, turning to the old man and pointing at the three sacred statues, 'the kingdom of our fathers is secure in its glory, but you have forgotten the fourth power that ruled over the world much earlier – all-embracing and unchallenged – you have forgotten the power of love.'

With these words he flung his arms round the neck of beautiful Lily. She had cast aside her veil and her cheeks blushed the most delicate immortal rose-red.

The old man laughed. 'Love does not rule but it educates and that is worth far more.' In the midst of all this joy and happiness, they had scarcely noticed the coming dawn. Now, with the sun high in the sky, those assembled were met with the sight of many rather unexpected objects as they looked through the open doorway. A huge square surrounded by columns formed a courtyard at the end of which was a splendid bridge that spanned the river with many arches. It had been conveniently and quite splendidly equipped on both sides with colonnades for those travelling on foot and there were already many thousands of these, passing busily to and fro. The great roadway in the middle was alive with livestock and mules, riders and carts, all of whom seemed to stream past each other in both directions without any trouble at all. Everyone marvelled at such ease and splendour and the new king and his bride were as delighted with the animation and activity before them as they were with their mutual love.

'Honour the serpent,' said the man with the lamp. 'You owe her your life and the people owe her this bridge, which now unites and brings life to these neighbouring shores. Those shining precious stones you saw floating in the water were all that remained of the body that she sacrificed. They now form the supports of this magnificent bridge, which built itself upon them and will never fall into disrepair.'

Further inquiry into the secrets behind this wonderful manifestation was hindered by the arrival of four beautiful maidens in the doorway of the temple. The presence of the harp, the parasol and the stool soon made it clear that they were none other than Lily's companions, but the identity of the fourth, more beautiful still than the others, remained a mystery as she hurried through the temple with them and climbed the silver stairs, joking all the while in a sisterly fashion.

'Will you now resolve to believe me in the future, dear wife?' the old man with the lamp asked the unknown beauty. 'How fortunate you are, as is every creature who goes to bathe in the river this morning!'

The old woman, now rejuvenated and quite beautiful, had kept nothing of her former appearance. She put her lithe, youthful arms round the man with the lamp, who happily returned her affectionate embrace.

'If I am too old for you,' he said, laughing, 'then you may choose a new husband today; from this day onwards no union is valid unless its vows have been renewed.'

'Do you not know that you have become younger too?' she replied.

'I am delighted that, in your eyes, I am once more a hearty young man; I take your hand anew and would happily live out the next thousand years with you.'

The queen welcomed her new friend and they both climbed up to the altar with her other companions while the king, accompanied by the other two men, looked over towards the bridge and observed with interest the swarming mass of people.

The king's pleasure was, however, short-lived, for he soon caught sight of something that gave cause for momentary concern. The great giant, who still seemed dazed after his morning sleep, came stumbling over the bridge, causing the greatest disarray as he did so. He was, as usual, still half asleep and clearly planned to bathe in his customary spot, but instead of water he found dry land and was forced to grope his way along the cobblestones of the bridge. Although his presence caused many to stop and stare as he trampled clumsily among both people and animals, no one seemed to feel it physically. As soon as the sun began to shine in his eyes, however, and he raised his hands to shade them, the shadow of his huge fists moved back and forth through the crowd with such cumbersome force that people and animals alike were thrown to the ground or injured; some barely escaped being flung into the river.

The king's immediate response as he witnessed this catastrophe was to reach for his sword, but then, having thought for a moment, his eyes were drawn first to his sceptre and then to the lamp and rudder held by his companions.

'I think I can guess your plan,' said the man with the lamp, 'but we and our powers can have no effect on the powerless. Stay calm! This is the last time he will cause such damage, and fortunately his shadow is turned away from us.'

Meanwhile, the giant had come ever closer and was utterly amazed by what he saw. His hands hung limply down and inflicted no more damage as he entered the courtyard open-mouthed.

He was just making his way to the doors of the temple when he found himself fixed to the ground in the middle of the courtyard. He stood like a colossal, mighty statue of gleaming red stone and his shadow marked the hours, which were laid out round him in a circle, not in the form of figures but instead in a series of lofty, meaningful symbols.

The king was quite delighted to see the shadow of the monster put to good use. The queen was no less amazed when she emerged, magnificently adorned, from the altar with her maidens and saw the strange statue that all but blocked the view of the bridge from the temple.

Meanwhile, the people had gathered in a circle around the motion-less giant and were marvelling at his sudden transformation. Then they turned towards the temple, which they seemed only just to have noticed, and thronged towards the doorway.

Just at that moment the hawk climbed high above the dome with the mirror, catching the sun's rays and directing the reflection on to the group by the altar. The king, the queen and her companions were all illuminated by a heavenly light, which lit up the dim vaults of the temple. The people fell to their knees before them. By the time the crowd had recovered and risen once more to its feet, the king and his party had already climbed down into the altar in order to cross the hidden halls to his palace. The curious people began to wander around in the temple. They beheld with wonder and reverence the three kings who stood before them, but were far more curious to discover what manner of lump lay hidden under a carpet in the fourth recess; for some unknown person had, in an act of well-meaning discretion, placed a rich cloth over the ruins of the fallen king through which no one could see and which no one was allowed to remove.

The people would most likely never have had enough of gazing and marvelling, and the prying mass might have crushed the very temple itself if attention had not been drawn once more outside to the great square.

A sudden shower of gold coins tumbled unexpectedly on to the marble slabs. Those nearest fell upon them greedily to secure them for themselves but then the miracle repeated itself, each time in a different place. The perpetrators of this prank were easily identified: the will-o'-the-wisps were having their parting fun, merrily squandering the gold from the limbs of the fallen king. The people ran greedily back and forth for a while longer, pushing and tearing at each other even after the gold coins had ceased to fall. Eventually, the crowd dispersed, each going their separate way. To this day the bridge still swarms with travellers and the temple is the most visited in the whole wide world.

Eckbert the Fair

LUDWIG TIECK

Deep in the Harz Mountains there lived a knight who was commonly known simply as Eckbert the Fair. He was some forty years old, little more than medium height with short, light blond hair that hung in a plain fashion, closely framing his pale, drawn face. He led a peaceful, solitary life, never becoming involved in his neighbours' quarrels, and was seldom seen beyond the boundary walls of his small castle. His wife was equally fond of such solitude, and they seemed to love each other dearly, yet they often bemoaned the fact that Heaven had not seen fit to bless their marriage with children.

Only rarely did Eckbert receive guests, and when any did come, then almost nothing of the daily rhythm of life was changed for their benefit. Moderation had made its home among them and Thrift itself seemed the rule of law. On such occasions Eckbert was merry and light-hearted, and it was only when he was alone that he displayed a certain air of reticence, one of silent, reserved melancholy.

No one visited the castle as often as Phillip Walther, a largely like-minded man to whom Eckbert had attached himself and of whom he was most fond. Walther actually lived in Franconia but often spent more than half the year in the vicinity of Eckbert's castle, gathering plants and stones and busying himself with their classification; he was in possession of a modest fortune and depended on no one. Eckbert often accompanied him on his lonely walks and over the years a deep friendship had grown between them.

There are times when it troubles a man to keep a secret from a friend, a secret which, until then, had been guarded with the utmost care; his soul is overcome by an irresistible desire to confide completely, to bare its innermost emotions to that friend, so that their friendship can become even closer. It might be the case, in such moments, that those more tender souls will come to appreciate one another more, yet, sometimes, it might also drive one party to shy away from acquaintance with the other.

It was already autumn when, on a misty evening, Eckbert sat with his friend and his wife at the fireside. The flames filled the chamber with a light glow and playfully lit the ceiling above; the black night peered in at the windows and the trees outside shivered in the damp cold. Walther complained of the long homeward journey that lay before him and Eckbert suggested that he stay, to spend half the night in companionable conversation and then to sleep until morning in a chamber in the castle. Walther fell in with this suggestion and wine and supper were served, the fire was stoked with wood and the friends' conversation grew merrier and more intimate.

Once the evening meal had been cleared away and the servants had once more withdrawn, Eckbert took Walther's hand and said, 'Dear friend, you must allow my wife to recount to you the tale of her youth – it is most odd.'

'A pleasure,' said Walther, and they all took their places once more round the hearth.

It had just turned midnight and every now and then the moon peered through the clouds that drifted overhead. 'You must not think me too forward,' began Bertha, 'my husband says that you are so noble of mind that it is wrong to hide anything from you. Yet, do not take my story for a fairy tale, however strange it may sound . . .

'I was born in a village. My father was a poor shepherd. My parents were very poor and often unsure where the next loaf of bread was coming from. What pained me far more was that my father and mother often quarrelled over their poverty and blamed one another bitterly. What was more, I constantly heard myself being called a simple, stupid child, incapable of carrying out even the most menial of tasks, and I was indeed utterly awkward and clumsy: I let everything fall from my fingers; I mastered neither sewing nor spinning; I could do nothing of use on the farm; and, indeed, my parents' poverty was all I had a real understanding for. I often sat in the corner and filled my head with ways to help them if I should suddenly become rich, how I would shower them with gold and silver and revel in their amazement. I conjured up spirits in my mind, who would show me hidden treasure or give me tiny pebbles that were transformed into precious stones. In short, the most wonderful fantasies preoccupied me and then, afterwards, when I had to get up to lend a hand or carry something, I seemed even more awkward, for my head still span with all these strange illusions.

'My father was always angry with me for being such a useless burden on the household. He often treated me rather cruelly and it was rare for me to hear a friendly word from him. Such had been my life when, at roughly the age of eight, serious efforts began to be made for me to do or learn something. My father believed it to be mere obstinacy or laziness on my part, to spend my days in idleness, and so he treated me even more harshly and set about me with quite unrepeatable threats. When these bore no fruit, he beat me in the most cruel way, saying that the punishment would be repeated every day, for I was little more than a useless creature.

'I wept bitterly the whole night through, I felt so completely abandoned and so sorry for myself that I wanted to die. I feared the break of day and simply did not know what course of action to take. I prayed for every skill imaginable and just could not understand why I was more simple than all the other children I knew. I was close to despair.

'As day dawned I rose, and, almost without knowing it, opened the door of our little hut. I found myself in the open field and soon after in a wood where the light of day could hardly be seen. I kept running onwards, without looking about me. I felt no fatigue, for I still believed my father would catch up with me, and, angered by my flight, treat me even more cruelly.

'When I emerged from the woods once more, the sun was quite high in the sky. I could see something dark in front of me, covered by a thick fog. First, I had to climb over hillocks, then follow a twisting path between cliffs, and it was then I guessed that I must be in the nearby mountains, the thought of which, in such solitude, made me feel quite afraid. While living on the plains I had never seen the mountains and when I heard people talk of them the mere mention of the word was quite terrifying to my child's ear. But I did not have the heart to turn back. My fear drove me on. I often looked round in fright when the wind rustled through the trees above or the distant sound of an axe chopping wood resounded through the morning silence. When, finally, I came across some charcoal burners and miners and heard their unfamiliar accent, I all but fainted in dismay.

'I passed through several villages, begging, for I was hungry and thirsty. I muddled through with excuses whenever I was questioned. I had travelled on like this for some four days when I came upon a small footpath, which took me ever further from the main highway. The cliffs around me then took on another, much stranger, appearance. There were crags so closely packed together that it looked as if the first gust of wind that came along would make them topple over. I did not know whether I should continue. At night I slept in the woods, for it was the mildest season of the year, or in remote shepherd's huts, but there was no human dwelling to be seen and I could not hope to find one in this wilderness. The cliffs became ever more fearsome and I often had to pass close to dizzying chasms. Eventually, even the path beneath my feet came to an end. Feeling quite disconsolate, I wept and cried out, my voice echoing back from the cliffs in a dreadful way. Night began to draw in and I looked for a mossy patch upon which to rest. I could not sleep for in the night I heard the most uncanny sounds; at first I thought they came from wild animals, then from the wind moaning through the cliffs, then from strange birds. I prayed and only much later, towards morning, did I fall asleep.

'I awoke as the day dawned. In front of me was a steep cliff, which I climbed in the hope of being able to spy from there an escape from the wilderness and perhaps even dwellings or people. Yet, as I stood at the top, everything as far as my eye could see, as well as everything around me, was covered in a misty haze. The day was grey and dull. I could not spy one tree, one meadow, not even one bush other than the lone miserable shrubs that had sprouted from the narrow cracks in the cliffs. It is impossible to describe the yearning I felt at that moment for the sight of another person, even if it were someone of whom I would have been afraid. At the same time I felt a torturous hunger. I sat down and made up my mind to die. After some time, however, the will to live won me over. I pulled myself to my feet and, in tears, carried on walking, sobbing intermittently, the whole day long. By the end I barely knew who I was. Tired and exhausted, I hardly wanted to live on, yet still I was afraid to die. Towards evening the surrounding countryside seemed to become somewhat friendlier and my thoughts and wishes were once more revived as the desire to live was reawakened in all my veins. I was convinced that I could hear the turning of a mill-wheel in the distance. I doubled my pace, and how relieved I was when I really did reach the end of the wild cliffs. I once more saw woods and meadows and distant mountains before me. It was as if I had come out of Hell and walked into Paradise. The isolation and my helplessness now no longer seemed at all frightening.

'Instead of the much-hoped-for mill, however, I came upon a waterfall, which of course greatly lessened my joy. As I scooped up a mouthful from the stream with my hand, I suddenly thought I could hear a soft coughing sound some distance away. Never have I been so pleasantly surprised as I was at that moment. I went closer and, at the edge of the wood, I could make out the form of an old woman, who seemed to be resting. She was dressed almost entirely in black, and a black hood covered her head and a large part of her face. In her hand she held a walking-stick.

'I approached her and asked for her help. She let me sit down at her side and gave me some bread and wine. While I ate, she sang a hymn in a screeching voice. When she had finished she asked me to follow her.

'I was most happy to follow this request, even though her voice and manner seemed rather odd to me. She moved fairly nimbly with her walking-stick and pulled such a face with every step that, at first, I had to laugh. The wild cliffs lay ever further behind us as we crossed a pleasant meadow and made our way through a rather dense wood. When we emerged, the sun was just setting, and I will never forget the sight and sensation I experienced that evening. Everything was blended into the softest red and gold. The trees stood with their tops brushing against the sunset and the fields were bathed in an enchanting glow. The woods and the leaves of the trees were still, and the clear sky resembled a beckoning Paradise. The bubbling of the springs and, from time to time, the whispering of the trees resounded through the clear calm as if singing of their melancholy joy. For the first time my young soul began to comprehend something of the world and all its wonders. I quite forgot myself and my guide as both spirit and eyes were lost in rapture among the golden clouds.

'We then climbed a small hill, which was planted with birch trees. From the top, the view looked over a green valley full of birches, and below, among the trees, there was a little hut. We were met with the sound of excited barking and soon a small lively dog appeared, jumping up at the old woman, wagging its tail. He then came to me, examined me from all sides, and returned happily to the old woman.

'As we walked down the hill, I heard wonderful singing that sounded like a bird and which seemed to come from the hut; it sang:

> ' "Lone woodland still,
> My constant thrill,
> You charm today
> And always will,
> My constant thrill
> Lone woodland still."

'These few words were repeated over and over again. If I were to describe it, I would say it was almost like the distant mingling of a French horn and a shawm.

'I was extremely curious and, without waiting for a sign from the old woman, I entered the hut. It was already twilight and everything was cleared away tidily. There were cups arranged on a wall cupboard and some strange receptacles stood on a table. A glittering cage with a bird in it hung by the window and, indeed, it was the bird who sang the words. The old lady wheezed and coughed, seeming unable to recover at all. She went to and fro, stroking the little dog and talking to the bird, whose only response was his customary song; for the most part she behaved as if I were not there at all. As I observed her, I could barely repress a shudder, for her features were constantly in motion as she nodded her head, as if from old age, so that I simply could not tell what she really looked like.

'Once she had recovered, she lit the lamp, laid a very small table and served the evening meal. At this point she looked round for me and told me to sit in one of the wicker chairs. I sat opposite her with the lamp between us. She folded her bony hands and prayed out loud, her face twitching all the time, so much so that I almost had to laugh again; but I restrained myself for I did not wish to anger her.

'After supper she prayed once more and then she showed me to a bed in a low, narrow chamber. She slept in the main room. Half numbed with fatigue, I did not remain awake for long, but I did wake a few times in the night and heard the old woman coughing and speaking to the dog, and occasionally to the bird who seemed to be dreaming, only ever singing a few words from his song. This, combined with the rustling of the birches at the window and the song of a distant nightingale, made such an odd mixture that it never felt as if I was awake but seemed instead as if I were sinking into another, even stranger, dream.

'In the morning the old woman woke me and soon afterwards set me to work. I was to spin, and this time I soon mastered it. I was also to care for the dog and the bird. I soon found my way around the household and the objects around me became familiar. By now it seemed to me that this was all as it should be, and I no longer felt that there was something odd about the old lady, nor that the house was unusual and rather isolated, nor that there was something extraordinary about the bird. I was, of course, always conscious of his beauty for his feathers shimmered with every possible colour. The loveliest pale blue and the fieriest red alternated on his neck and body and when he sang he puffed out with pride so that his feathers were more impressive than ever.

'Often the old woman would go out and not return until evening. When she did I would go to meet her with the dog and she would call me "child" and "daughter". With the passing of time I grew quite fond of her, growing accustomed to her in the way the mind accustoms itself to everything, especially in childhood. In the evenings she taught me to read. I mastered the art with ease and later it became a source of endless pleasure to me in my solitude for she had in her possession a few old handwritten books full of marvellous stories.

'The memories of my life back then still seem strange to me now; never visited by another living soul, being part of such a small family circle. Indeed, I felt for the dog and the bird as I might otherwise feel towards long-standing friends. I have never been able to remember the strange name the dog had, despite having called him by it so often.

'I had been living with the old woman like this for four years and must have been almost twelve years old when she finally trusted me enough to reveal a secret to me. Every day the bird laid an egg, which contained a pearl or a jewel. I had certainly noticed that she dealt with the cage in secret but had never really concerned myself with it any further. She now gave me the task of removing the eggs in her absence, and of keeping them safe in the odd receptacles. She left me food and stayed away for longer periods – weeks or even months. My spinning-wheel hummed, the dog barked, the wonderful bird sang and, meantime, everything was so calm around us that I cannot recall there having been a single high wind or storm the whole time I was there. No one ever strayed our way, no animals ever came near our dwelling. I was content and worked on from one day to the next. – Perhaps people would be truly happy if they could live out their lives like this, undisturbed, until the end.

'From the little that I read, I created a wondrous image in my mind of the world and its people. Everything was inspired by my own situation. When it came to happy people, I could not imagine anything other than the little dog. Splendid ladies always resembled the bird and old women looked like my own wondrous old woman. I had also read a little on the subject of love and span wonderful tales for myself in my imagination. I imagined the handsomest knight in the world, I endowed him with every desirable trait imaginable, without actually knowing how he might look after all my efforts. Indeed, I often felt truly sorry for myself when he did not return my love and would deliver wrought speeches in my thoughts, sometimes even out loud, in order just to win him over. – You may laugh! We are all now, of course, beyond that stage of youth.

'I now much preferred to be alone, for then I was the mistress of the house. The dog loved me very much and did everything I wanted. The bird responded to all my questions with his song, my spinning-wheel turned merrily and I truly felt no desire for change. When-ever the old woman returned from her long journeys, she would praise my care and attention. She said that since my joining it, her household was far more orderly. She took pleasure in seeing me grow and in my healthy appearance and, in short, treated me just like a daughter.

' "You are a good girl, my child!" she once said to me in her rough voice. "If you continue this way, you will always do well: yet no one ever prospers if they stray from the true path: punishment will follow, no matter how late." – I was not really paying much heed while she was saying this, for I was a very lively child in all aspects of my character; but it came back to me later that night and I could not understand what she had meant by it. I considered all the words carefully. I had, of course, read of riches and eventually it occurred to me that her pearls and jewels could probably be of some value. This became increasingly clear to me. But whatever did she mean by the true path? I still could not quite grasp the meaning of her words.

'By then I was fourteen years old and it is unfortunate for humanity that wisdom is gained only at the expense of an innocent soul. For it had become clear to me that all I had to do was take the bird and the treasures while the old woman was away and make off with them in search of the world of which I had read. After all, it might even be possible for me to meet that handsome knight who was still ever-present in my mind.

'To begin with, this notion seemed of no more importance than any other but, whenever I sat there at my wheel, it would come back to me against my will, and I would lose myself in thought to the extent that I could already see myself beautifully bedecked in jewels with knights and princes all around me. Whenever I forgot myself like this, it distressed me terribly to look up and find myself in the little house. What was more, when I went about my daily tasks, the old woman did not concern herself with what I was doing.

'One day my hostess set off again and informed me that this time she would stay away longer than usual. I was to look after everything properly and not waste my time. I bid her farewell with a certain degree of apprehension for it felt as if I would never see her again. I stood watching her go for a long time and was myself unsure as to why I felt so afraid. It was almost as if my intentions already lay mapped out without really being clear to me.

'Never had I cared for the dog and the bird with such zeal; they were dearer to me than ever before. The old woman had already been gone for several days when I awoke with the firm intention of taking the bird and leaving the hut to seek out the so-called world. My thoughts were oppressive and troubled me greatly. I wanted to stay on there but yet the very thought repulsed me. There was a strange battle in my soul, like the struggle between two opposing spirits within me. One minute the peaceful isolation seemed quite beautiful to me, the next I was enticed by the prospect of a new world with all its wonderful variety.

'I did not know what to make of myself. The dog sprang up at me incessantly, the sunshine spread out happily over the fields and the green birch trees shimmered. Sensing I had something very pressing to do, I seized the little dog and tied him up in the room. Then I took down the cage with the bird in and put it under my arm. The dog cowered and whined, unaccustomed to such treatment. He looked at me with pleading eyes but I was afraid to take him with me. I then took one of the vessels filled with jewels and placed it in my apron. The rest I left where they were.

'The bird moved his head around in a strange fashion as I carried him through the door. The dog strained in anguish, trying to follow me, but he had to stay behind.

'I avoided the path that led to the wild cliffs and went the opposite way. The dog was still barking and whimpering and my heart truly bled for him. The bird tried once or twice to strike up his song but, as I was carrying him, he seemed reluctant to do so.

'As I walked on the sound of barking became weaker and finally it stopped altogether. I wept and almost turned back but the deep desire to experience something new drove me onwards.

'I had already crossed the mountains and passed through several forests when evening fell and I had to make for a village inn. I felt rather unsure of myself as I entered the tavern. I was shown to a room with a bed, where I slept quite peacefully except when I found myself dreaming of the old woman threatening me.

'My journey was rather tedious but the further I went the more the thought of the old woman and the little dog frightened me. I realized that without my help he would probably starve to death. In the forest I often imagined I saw the old woman suddenly coming towards me. Plagued by these thoughts, sighing tearfully, I continued on my way. Every time I rested and placed the cage on the ground the bird would sing his wondrous song and each time I could clearly picture the beautiful remote place we had once lived in. Human nature being wont to forget, I now imagined my previous journey in childhood to have been far less miserable than the one I now endured; I wished I were in the same position again.

'I had sold a few jewels and, having journeyed for many days, I came to a village. The moment I entered it, I had an odd feeling but did not know why. I soon realized why, however, for it was the selfsame village in which I had been born. How surprised I was! How the tears of joy ran down my cheeks at the recollection of a thousand strange memories! Much had changed; there were new houses, others which had just been built when I lived there had fallen into disrepair, and I came upon burnt-out ruins too. Everything was much smaller and more cramped than I had expected. I felt boundless pleasure at the prospect of seeing my parents once more after so many years. I found the little house with its old familiar threshold. The door handle was exactly the same as before and it felt like only yesterday that I had closed it behind me. My heart pounded impetuously as I hastily opened the door – but the faces of those sitting around the room, staring at me, were those of strangers. I asked after the old shepherd Martin and they told me that he had died some three years ago along with his wife. – I withdrew hastily and left the village weeping aloud.

'I had long imagined how wonderful it would be to surprise them with my riches and now, quite by chance, my childhood dream had come true – and yet it was all in vain. They could no longer share my happiness with me and the one thing I had hoped for most in life was lost to me for ever.

'I took a small house with a garden in a pleasant town and hired a serving maid. The world had not impressed me as much as I had expected but I gradually forgot about the old woman and my previous home and, on the whole, I lived quite contentedly.

'The bird had not sung for a long time. I was, therefore, more than a little startled when he began to sing again one evening. This time the song was different. He sang:

> ' "Lone woodland still,
> How far your hills,
> Repentance stirs,
> In time it fills,
> How far your hills,
> Lone woodland still."

'I was unable to sleep all night. Everything came back to me and, more than ever, I felt I had done something wrong. As I rose, the sight of the bird repulsed me. He kept looking over at me and his presence frightened me. He would not stop singing his song and sang louder and more resoundingly than ever before. The more I watched him, the more nervous he made me. Finally, I opened the cage, put my hand in and took hold of his neck. I pressed my fingers together firmly. He looked at me, his eyes pleading, and I let go, but he was already dead. – I buried him in the garden.

'From then on I often felt afraid of my servant. I thought of my own actions and of how she in turn could rob or even murder me. – For some time I had known a young knight whom I liked very much. I gave him my hand and, with that, Walther, my story is at an end.'

'You ought to have seen her then,' added Eckbert hastily. 'Her youth, her beauty and – what mysterious charm her solitary upbringing had blessed her with. She seemed like a miracle to me and I loved her beyond all measure. I had no fortune – this wealth came with her love. We moved here and have not, to this day, ever had cause to regret our union – not even for one moment.'

'But what chatterboxes we are,' said Bertha. 'It is the middle of the night – we ought to retire to bed.'

She rose to her feet and made to leave for her bedchamber. Walther bid her good-night, placed a kiss on her hand as he did so, and said, 'Noble lady, I thank you, I can clearly picture you with that marvellous bird, feeding little *Strohmian*.'

Walther too retired to bed. Only Eckbert remained, pacing the hall uneasily. – 'Is man not foolish?' he said to himself at last. 'It was at my own bidding that my wife told Walther her tale to begin with but now I regret the confidence! – Will he not abuse it? Will he not tell others? Will he not perhaps – for it is in man's nature – covet our precious jewels with soulless greed and then make secret plans to steal them?'

It occurred to him that Walther had not taken leave of him with quite the warmth one would have expected after hearing such a confidence. Once the soul has begun to harbour suspicion, the notion soon spreads, finding confirmation in the smallest of details. Eckbert reproached himself for this base mistrust of his loyal friend but yet could not quite put it out of his mind. He tossed and turned, plagued by these thoughts all through the night, and slept very little.

Bertha was unwell and unable to come down for breakfast. Walther seemed most unconcerned at this and parted from the knight with equal indifference. Eckbert could not fathom his behaviour. He visited his wife. She lay in a fever and said that the recounting of her tale the night before must have strained her.

From that evening onwards, Walther did not visit his friend's castle very often, and when he did come he left again after making only a few trivial remarks. Eckbert was tormented in the extreme by this behaviour. He hid it, of course, from Bertha and Walther, but his inner agitation must have been obvious to anyone.

Bertha's illness caused ever more concern and the physician feared for her life. The colour had drained from her cheeks and her fevered eyes were burning. – One morning she sent for her husband to come to her bedside and the maids were sent away. 'Dear husband,' she began, 'I must tell you something which, as unimportant a detail as it might seem, has all but driven me insane and greatly affected my health. – You know that whenever I spoke of my childhood, I could never, despite every effort, remember the name of the little dog whose company I enjoyed for so long. That evening, as he bade me good-night, Walther suddenly said to me, "I can clearly picture you feeding little *Strohmian.*" Is it a coincidence? Did he guess the name, did he know it and mention it with some intent? And how is this man linked to my fate? I keep struggling with myself, trying to convince myself that I am imagining this oddity, but it is real, simply too real. I was overcome with unspeakable terror to hear a stranger aid my memory in this way. What do you think, Eckbert?'

Eckbert looked at his suffering wife, deeply moved. He was silent and thought for a moment, then he said a few comforting words and left her. In a remote chamber of the castle he paced up and down in indescribable agitation. Walther had been his only companion for many years and yet this person was now the only one in the world whose existence threatened and tormented him. It seemed he would be at ease once more only if this one individual could be cleared from his path. Seeking some form of distraction, he took down his crossbow and set out to hunt.

It was a raw, stormy winter's day. Deep snow covered the mountains and bent the branches on the trees down to the ground. Eckbert wandered around, beads of sweat on his brow. He shot no game and this worsened his mood. Suddenly he saw something moving in the distance. It was Walther gathering moss from the trees. Without realizing what he was doing, Eckbert took aim. Walther looked round and threatened with a silent gesture, but at that moment the bolt flew from the bow and Walther fell to the ground.

Eckbert felt relieved and reassured, yet a cold fear drove him back towards his castle. He had a long way to go, for he had strayed deep into the forest. – By the time he arrived, Bertha had already passed away. Before her death she had spoken a great deal about Walther and the old woman.

Thereafter Eckbert lived for a long time in the greatest solitude.

He had long been melancholy in nature, for his wife's strange story troubled him deeply and he had always feared some unhappy event, but now he was quite at odds with himself. The murder of his friend was forever on his mind and he lived with continual self-reproach.

In an attempt to amuse himself, he occasionally ventured to the nearest large town, where he attended gatherings and celebrations. He hoped to fill the emptiness through some new acquaintance or another. Yet, whenever he thought of Walther anew, he was filled with fear at the prospect of finding a new friend, for he was convinced that he could only be unhappy, no matter who that friend might be. He had lived for such a long time in peaceful harmony with Bertha; the friendship with Walther had brought him so much happiness over the years; and now both had been carried off so suddenly that at times his life seemed more akin to a strange fairy tale than reality.

A young knight by the name of Hugo befriended the silent, troubled Eckbert and seemed to be truly fond of him. Eckbert was most pleasantly surprised and returned the knight's friendship all the more readily, having expected it so little. The pair were now often together and the stranger showed Eckbert every possible favour. The one now hardly ever rode out without the other. They met at every gathering and seemed inseparable.

Yet, Eckbert was only ever happy for brief moments at a time, for he was sure that Hugo must be mistaken in his love for him. He did not know him; he did not know his story; and Eckbert was plagued by the same compulsion to tell Hugo everything so that he could be sure of his friendship, but then he was once more held back by anxiety and the fear of rejection. There were moments when he was so utterly convinced of his worthlessness that he believed no person to whom he was not a complete stranger could grant him their respect. Still, he could not contain himself. While out on a lonely ride, Eckbert recounted his whole story to his friend and then asked him if he could truly love a murderer. Hugo was moved and tried to comfort him. Eckbert followed him back to town with a lighter heart.

Yet Eckbert seemed doomed to harbour suspicion from the very moment his trust had been placed, for hardly had he entered the hall than he sensed displeasure in the faces of his friends under the glare of the many lights. He was sure that Hugo's smile was mocking him; he began to notice that Hugo seemed to be avoiding him while paying far more heed to the other guests. Among the assembled company there was an old knight who had always made a point of opposing Eckbert and who had often inquired after his riches and his wife in a rather peculiar manner. Hugo sought him out and the pair spoke secretly together for some time, pointing to Eckbert as they did so. The latter now had his suspicions confirmed; he thought he had been betrayed and a terrible anger possessed him. As he continued to stare across at them, he suddenly saw Walther's face – all his features, his entire, all-too-familiar, figure. Eckbert continued to stare and was convinced that it was none other than Walther himself talking to the old man. – His horror was indescribable. Beside himself, he rushed outside. He left the town that very night and returned, after losing his way many times, to his castle.

Once there, Eckbert rushed from room to room like a restless spirit, unable to compose himself at all. His mind lurched from one dreadful thought to another, horror mounting on horror; he could not sleep a wink. He often felt that he must be insane and that everything was simply a wild figment of his imagination. Then he would remember Walther's features again and everything became even more of a mystery to him. He decided to go on a journey in an attempt to bring his thoughts into order. The notion of friendship, the desire for human contact, were abandoned for ever.

Eckbert set off with no particular route in mind. Indeed he paid scant attention to the landscape before him. Having ridden on in haste for a few days at full pelt, he suddenly found he had strayed into a labyrinth of cliffs from which there appeared to be no means of escape. Eventually, he met a peasant who showed him a path across a waterfall. Eckbert wanted to give him a few coins to show his gratitude but the peasant refused. – 'What does it matter?' Eckbert said to himself. 'I could almost begin to imagine him to be none other than Walther' –

And with that he looked round and saw that it was indeed none other than Walther. – Eckbert spurred on his steed as fast as it could run, through meadows and woods, until it collapsed exhausted beneath him. – Unperturbed by this, he continued his journey on foot. As if in a dream, he climbed a hill. He thought he could make out the sound of excited barking near by, birches rustled in the background and he heard the words of a song being sung in wonderful tones:

> 'Lone woodland still,
> Again my thrill,
> No envy stirs,
> No hate can kill,
> Again my thrill,
> Lone woodland still.'

Eckbert's reason, his senses, were now spent. He could find no answer to the mystery – was he dreaming now, or had he been dreaming before, of a woman called Bertha? Wondrous things were mixed with the most ordinary. The world around him seemed to be bewitched and he was powerless to think or remember.

A crooked old woman, leaning on a stick and coughing, approached the mound stealthily. 'Have you brought my bird? My pearls? My dog?' she screamed at him. 'You see, wrong brings its own punishment: your friend Walther, your Hugo – they were none other than me.'

'God in Heaven,' Eckbert whispered to himself. 'What awful solitude have I been living in!'

'And Bertha was your sister.'

Eckbert sank to the ground.

'Why did she leave me so treacherously? Everything would have turned out well otherwise. The period of her trial was already over. She was the daughter of a knight who had her brought up by a shepherd – your father's child.'

'Why did I always fear something as terrible as this?' cried Eckbert.

'Because as a young child you once heard your father speak of it; he was not allowed to bring this daughter up at home because of his wife, for the child was born of another woman.'

Eckbert lay crazed and dying on the ground; his mind dulled and confused, he heard the old woman speaking, the dog barking and the bird singing its song over and over again.

Undine

FRIEDRICH DE LA MOTTE FOUQUÉ

CHAPTER I

How the Knight Came upon the Fisherman

Many hundreds of years ago an old fisherman sat one evening in the doorway of his hut, mending his nets. The place where he lived was really quite idyllic; the lush land upon which his hut was built jutted out into a vast lake, stretching out into the wonderfully clear blue waters as if besotted by them. The waves too reached out with loving arms to embrace the beautiful meadow with its tall waving grasses and flowers and the refreshing shade of its trees. They were together as one and it was this harmony that made everything there so beautiful. Yet, very few people, apart from the fisherman and his family, frequented this charming place, for behind the strip of land there lay a deep wild forest, which most people did not dare enter, except in cases of extreme necessity, for fear of its impenetrable darkness and the strange creatures and phantoms that were said to lurk there. Yet the God-fearing old fisherman traversed it quite regularly without incident on his way to and from the large city, which lay just beyond the great wood, as he took the delicious fish he caught to market. His journey was no doubt made all the easier by the fact that an unworthy thought never entered his head, and, each time the dreaded shadows approached, he would strike up a hymn and sing from the bottom of his heart and at the top of his voice.

As he sat there innocently that evening, mending his nets, he was startled to hear a rustling sound akin to that of a man on horseback coming from the dark depths of the wood. The noise seemed to be coming closer and closer and the dreams he had often had on stormy nights, dreams of the secrets of the forest, flashed through his mind, above all the image of an incredibly tall snow-white man whose head nodded incessantly in the strangest manner. Indeed, as the fisherman looked towards the forest, he thought he could see the nodding man approaching through the veil of leaves. He soon gathered his senses, however, reasoning that nothing untoward had ever happened to him in the forest itself, and that the evil spirit would, therefore, have even less power over him out in the open. All the same, he prayed with a sense of urgency, uttering aloud words from the Bible that revived his failing courage, and, indeed, he almost laughed when he saw how wrong he had been, for all at once he recognized the white nodding man as a familiar old stream that gushed out from the forest into the lake. The cause of the noise, it appeared, had been a magnificently clad knight, who now rode through the shadows towards the hut. A scarlet cloak was draped over his violet, gold-embroidered doublet; red and violet feathers flowed from a gold-coloured cap; a quite beautiful and richly adorned sword hung, gleaming, from a golden armour belt. The white stallion that carried the knight was rather more finely built than is usually the case with battle horses and stepped so lightly over the grass that the green, mottled carpet seemed to suffer no injury whatsoever. The old fisherman was still uneasy, although he felt sure that such a fair apparition could bring no harm, and so politely doffed his cap at the approaching gentleman as he stood calmly beside his nets. The knight drew up and asked if he might request shelter overnight for himself and his horse. 'As far as your horse is concerned, dear sir,' replied the fisherman; 'I know of no better stable to recommend than this shady meadow and no better fodder than the grass that grows there. As for your good self, I would be pleased to offer you the best food and shelter that my little house can offer.' The knight was well pleased with this. He dismounted and the pair then relieved the horse of its tack and let it run out on to the flower-strewn grass.

Turning to his host, the knight said, 'Had I found you less hospitable and well-meaning, my dear old fisherman, then you would still not have been rid of me today, for I see there is a great lake before us, and to ride back into the strange wood at sunset – God preserve me from that!'

'Let us not dwell on such things,' said the fisherman and led his guest into the hut.

Inside, on a large chair by the hearth, sat the fisherman's wife. A meagre fire gave out a dim light, which barely illuminated the neatly kept room. The old woman stood up to welcome the noble guest as he entered but then sat down again in her place of honour without offering it to the stranger. Smiling, the fisherman said, 'Do not be offended, young sir, if she does not offer you the most comfortable chair in the house; it is custom among poor people to reserve such privileges for the old.'

'Oh, husband,' said the woman with a patient smile, 'what a thing to say! Our guest is a good Christian, is he not? And how could such a young man even think of chasing an old woman from her chair?'

'Sit down, young man,' she continued, turning to the knight. 'There is a quite comfortable little chair over there, only take care not to handle it too roughly; one of the legs is not as firm as it once was.' The knight fetched the chair with great care and sat down good-humouredly, feeling quite at home, as if he truly belonged at the heart of this little household and had just returned there from afar.

And so, the three good people began to converse companionably and convivially with one another. The old man would not be drawn on the matter of the woods, even though the knight inquired about it several times; it was particularly inappropriate to talk of it as night fell, he said; the couple were, however, far more forthcoming about their livelihood and daily activities and listened with interest as the knight told them of his travels, of his castle at the source of the Danube and his name: Sir Huldbrand von Ringstetten. Half-way through the conversation the stranger became aware of a splashing noise at one of the low windows, as if someone were spraying water at it. The old man grimaced irritably each time the noise was heard; when, however, a whole jet of water flew against the glass and sprayed into the room through the poorly fashioned sill, he stood up angrily and shouted threateningly at the window: 'Undine! Will you stop these childish games once and for all. We have a visitor in the hut this night, you know.' There was silence outside with only a stifled giggle to be heard. Returning to the hearth, the fisherman said, 'You will just have to ignore that, my honoured guest, and I dare say a few more such indiscretions besides, but she means no ill. That was our ward, Undine, who refuses to grow out of these childish ways even though she is about to turn eighteen. But as I said, in truth, she is good at heart.'

'That is easy for you to say!' replied the old woman, shaking her head. 'When you come back from fishing or from a journey, then her pranks might seem quite endearing. But when you have her under your feet all day long and hear not a sensible word and, instead of having more help in the house as she gets older, are forced to ensure that her follies do not bring an end to us altogether – then it is quite another matter, which would try the patience of an angel.'

'Now, now,' her husband smiled, 'you have Undine to deal with, I have the lake. It often pulls down my causeways and tears my nets, but I still love it, just as you love the delicate child, despite all the bother and misery. Is it not so?'

'You cannot be really angry with her, it is true,' said the old woman, and she smiled approvingly.

Just then the door flew open and a wondrously beautiful young girl with golden hair appeared, and said with a laugh, 'You are making fun of me, father; where is our guest then?' At the same moment she noticed the knight and stopped, staring in amazement at the handsome young man. Huldbrand was captivated by the lovely figure and wanted to take in the pretty features fully, for he was sure that only this moment of surprise would allow him time to do so and that, once recovered, she would shy away from him in deep embarrassment. Things happened quite differently, however, for once she had looked him over at some length, she stepped confidently closer, knelt before him and began playing with a golden medallion, which hung from a rich chain at his breast. 'Oh most beautiful, most welcome guest,' she said, 'how did you come upon our poor hut? Did you have to wander in the world for years before you found your way to us? Do you come from the wild wood, my handsome friend?' The old woman's reproaches left him no time to answer. She ordered the girl to stand up, mind her manners and go about her work. Undine did not respond but instead pulled up a small footstool next to Huldbrand's chair and sat down with her needlework. 'I want to work here,' she said amiably.

The old man did as the parents of spoilt children are wont to do: he pretended not to have noticed Undine's misbehaviour and began to talk about something else. But the girl would not let him. She said, 'I asked our fair guest where he has come from and he has not yet answered me.'

'From the forest, dear child,' replied Huldbrand.

'Then,' she continued, 'you must tell us how you came to be there, for people generally shy away from it; and tell us too what strange adventures you had, for they say it is impossible to go there without experiencing something.' Huldbrand felt a slight shiver as he remembered and looked involuntarily towards the window, fearing that one of the strange figures he had met in the forest might be grinning in at him; but outside he saw nothing more than the deep black night that had now fallen beyond the window-panes. He then composed himself and was about to begin his tale when the old man interrupted him:

'No, sir; this is not the right time.'

Undine leapt angrily from her stool, thrust her beautiful hands on her hips and, standing close up to the fisherman, shouted at the top of her voice, 'Not the right time? Not now? But I want him to tell; he must! He simply must!' Her tiny foot stamped the ground with an air of such comical, endearing righteousness that Huldbrand was even less able to take his eyes from her in her anger than he had been before. The old man, however, was beside himself with rage and scolded Undine severely for her disobedience and impolite behaviour towards the stranger. The old woman agreed with him heartily. Undine retorted with equal vehemence, 'If you can do nothing but scold me and refuse to grant my will then you can sleep alone in your old smoky hut!' With that, she flew through the door like an arrow and ran out into the dark night.

CHAPTER 2

How Undine Came to be with the Fisherman

Huldbrand and the fisherman sprang from their seats and made to go after the irate girl, but even before they could reach the doorway of the hut Undine had vanished into the murky darkness beyond. Not even the sound of her light footsteps betrayed the direction in which she had flown. Perplexed, the knight turned to his host; it seemed as if the entire captivating vision, which had vanished all at once into the darkness, had been little more than another of the strange phantoms that had earlier tormented Huldbrand in the forest, but the old man muttered between his teeth, 'It is not the first time that she has treated us in this way. Now we shall have fear in our hearts and not a wink of sleep the whole night long; for who knows whether or not she will come to harm if she stays out there alone in the darkness until daybreak.'

'Then let us go after her, for God's sake!' cried Huldbrand anxiously.

'Where is the good in that?' the old man replied. 'It would be a sin if I were to let you chase after the thoughtless girl alone through the lonely night and, even if we did know which way she had gone, my old legs no longer have the strength to catch such a young fly-by-night.'

'Then we must at least call after her and beg her to come back,' said Huldbrand; and he began to call out to her, his voice filled with emotion, 'Undine! Oh, Undine! Please come back!' The old man shook his head, saying that all the shouting would be to no avail; the knight had no idea how stubborn the youngster was. All the same he could not help but join in, calling out into the dark night over and over again: 'Undine! Oh dear Undine! I beg you, come back just this once.'

It was, however, as the fisherman had said it would be. There was no sign of Undine and, because the old man refused to allow Huldbrand to trail the vanished girl, they both eventually had to return to the hut. Here they found the fire all but extinguished in the grate. The housewife, who had not taken Undine's disappearance and likely danger nearly so much to heart as her husband, had already gone to bed. The old man raked over the coals, laid some dry wood on top and, as the flames took hold once more, fetched a jug of wine, which he placed between himself and his guest. 'You fear for the silly girl too, sir,' he said, 'so we may as well spend some of the night chatting and drinking, rather than tossing and turning on a mattress of straw, trying in vain to sleep; am I not right?' Huldbrand consented willingly. The old man gestured to him to sit in the place of honour left vacant by the sleeping housewife and so they drank and conversed as befits two worthy and trusty men. Of course, each time there was the slightest movement outside the window, or even if there was none, one or other of the two would look up and say, 'She is coming.' Then they would sit for a few moments in silence and when nothing appeared, they would carry on their conversation with a shake of the head and a sigh.

As neither of them was capable of thinking of anything other than Undine, there seemed nothing better than for the knight to hear how Undine came to be with the old fisherman. He began his tale thus:

'Some fifteen years hence, I was making my way through the wild forest to the city to sell my wares. My wife had stayed at home as usual, except at that time there were very good grounds for her to do so, for although we were both getting on in years, even then, God had blessed us with a beautiful child. It was a little girl and we were already discussing whether we ought not perhaps make plans to leave our lovely strip of land for the sake of the new arrival in order to give this gift from Heaven a better upbringing in a more hospitable place. Poor people are not always able to do as you might think they should in such cases, dear sir, but with the Lord's help, we must all do the best we can! These were the thoughts going round in my head as I went. I loved our strip of land so much and the city, with all its clamour and brawling, made me feel quite uneasy. I thought to myself: do you really want to move your loved ones to somewhere as unruly as this or perhaps even worse? – Even so, I did not grumble to God but silently thanked him all the more for the new-born child. It would be a lie, too, if I were to say that on my journey to town or back home that day, I had come across anything out of the ordinary, for I had never seen anything untoward in the forest. The Lord was ever by my side in those mysterious shadows.'

He took the little cap from his bald head and sat still for a short while in prayer. Then he replaced his cap and continued:

'But, alas, on this side of the forest sorrow awaited me. My wife came to meet me, tears streaming down her face. She was dressed in mourning. "Oh dear God," I groaned, "Where is our beloved child? Tell me." "Dear husband, she is with the Lord whose name you call," she replied and we went to the hut together, weeping silently. I looked around for the tiny corpse; only then did I discover what had happened. My wife had been sitting at the lakeside with the child and, as she played with her there, quite innocently and happily, the child suddenly leaned forward as if attracted by something wondrous in the water. My wife saw her laughing, the dear angel, and grasping with her hands; then all at once the child slipped from her arms and plunged into the watery mirror below. I looked for a long time for the little corpse but it was no use; there was no trace of her to be found.

'Two bereaved parents sat together that night in the hut; neither of us would have felt like talking, even if our tears had permitted it. So we sat staring into the fire in the grate. Suddenly there was a rustling noise at the door. It sprang open and a beautiful girl of some three or four years of age, dressed in fine clothes, stood on the doorstep, smiling at us. We were utterly dumbfounded and at first I did not know whether it was a real little person or a mere phantom. Then I noticed the water that was dripping from her golden hair and rich clothes and realized that the beautiful child had been lying in the water and was in need of help. "Wife," I said, "no one was able to save our child but now we have the chance to do for others the one thing which would have made us so happy on this earth." We undressed the little girl, put her to bed and gave her drinks to warm her up, during all of which she uttered not one word but just kept staring at us with her sea-blue eyes, smiling all the while.

'The next morning we were able to satisfy ourselves that she had come to no further harm and so I asked her about her parents and how she came to be there. This elicited a muddled, rather odd response. She must have been born far away for I have been unable these fifteen years to discover anything of her origin; she said – and still says – such strange things now and then, that we are not sure whether, in the end, she might just as well have come down to us from the moon. There is talk of golden castles, glass ceilings and Lord knows what else. The clearest thing she was able to relate was that she had gone out on the great lake with her mother, fallen from the boat and only recovered her senses under the trees on the welcoming shore, where she soon felt at ease.

'There were many questions to consider and much concern in our hearts. It was soon agreed that we should keep and raise the little foundling in place of the child we had lost; but how were we to know whether or not she had been baptized? She was herself unable to enlighten us. She would often respond to our questions by saying that she knew she had been created for the glory of God, and that we must do with her whatever would please and honour the Lord. My wife and I decided, if she has not been baptized then there is no time to waste; if she has, then too much of a good thing is surely better than too little. So then we began to think of a suitable name for the child, whose true name we still did not know. We finally decided on Dorothea as the name most suited to her, for I had once heard that it meant "a gift from God", and she had indeed been sent to us by God as a gift to comfort us in our misery. She, however, would hear nothing of it and told us that, as her parents had called her Undine, Undine she would remain. I was sure this was a heathen name, not to be found in any calendar, and so I sought the advice of a priest in the city. He would not hear of her keeping the name Undine either but, after much persuasion, agreed to come with me through the strange forest to perform the baptism ceremony here in my little hut. The little one stood there before us, so charmingly clad and innocent, that the priest soon lost his heart to her. She flattered him so sweetly while at the same time contradicting him so comically that, in the end, he could no longer remember what grounds he had against the name Undine in the first place. So she was baptized Undine and was as well-behaved and sweet during the formal ceremony as she was normally wild and naughty. For my wife was quite right, we have had a great deal to put up with her. I could tell you a few tales –'

The knight interrupted him to draw his attention to a noise which sounded like the violent cascading of water, which he had begun to notice during the old man's tale. It was now hammering against the windows of the hut with increasing ferocity. They both rushed to the door. Outside, in a shaft of clear moonlight, they saw that the stream that ran from the forest had burst its banks with quite vicious force, propelling stones and tree trunks along with it. Just then the storm broke above them, as if awoken by the crashing sound, chasing the great clouds across the moon; the lake howled, whipped by the beating wings of the wind; on the strip of land the trees groaned from root to tip, bent as if reeling over the ripping waters. 'Undine! For God's sake, Undine!' cried the two terrified men. There was no reply and, now oblivious to every other consideration, they ran from the hut in opposite directions, searching and shouting.

CHAPTER 3

How They Found Undine Again

Huldbrand became ever more anxious and confused the longer they searched in vain through the shadows of the night. The thought that Undine had been nothing more than a vision, a trick played by the forest, once more began to dominate his mind. Indeed, so complete was the metamorphosis of this once so peaceful place – the howling waves, the raging storm and the crashing trees – that the entire strip of land including the hut and its inhabitants might well have been just a deceitful apparition. Yet, in the distance, he could still hear the anxious cries of the fisherman as he called out for Undine, accompanied by the voice of the old woman, which rang out in prayer and song through the terrible roar. Just then Huldbrand came to the edge of the flooded stream. In the moonlight he could see it had driven its unruly path along the edge of the mysterious forest, turning the peninsula into an island. Oh dear God, he thought to himself, what if Undine has dared to step even a little way into that terrible forest;

she might well have been stubborn enough to do such a thing just because I would not tell her about it – and, now that the stream has cut her off, what if she is alone over there, weeping and surrounded by ghoulish spirits! A cry of horror escaped from his lips. He clambered over stones and fallen pine trees towards the wild torrent in an attempt to wade or swim across to search for the lost girl. Now, amid the rustling and howling of branches, everything he had seen earlier that day seemed gruesome and uncanny. In particular, there was a tall white man – all too familiar to him already – who stood, grinning and nodding on the opposite bank. Yet, it was these very monstrous images that drove him onwards, for he was afraid that Undine might be among them, alone and in fear of her life.

Barely able to keep himself upright against the force of the swirling flood waters, he had already seized hold of a sturdy branch to use for support and stood in the raging stream; then, his courage renewed, he strode further in. All at once, he heard a charming voice next to him: 'Do not trust him, do not trust him! He is treacherous, the old man, the stream!'

Huldbrand recognized the sweet sound and stood as if bewitched in the dark shadows that had just drawn across the moon. He felt giddy at the sight of the rolling waves, which swirled around his thighs, but refused to give up. 'If you are not really there, if you are nothing but a fleeting shadow in the mist, then I no longer wish to live but instead to become a shadow just like you, my dear, dear Undine!' he cried aloud as he stepped further into the torrent.

A voice close by his side cried out: 'Look round, will you, just look round, my dear handsome, enraptured young friend!' Looking to the side as the moonlight emerged once more, Huldbrand saw Undine on a little island which had been created by the flood. She was smiling and nestled coyly in the lush grass under the branches of the overhanging trees.

Oh, how much more joyfully the young man made use of his pine stave than before! In a few steps he had crossed the flood waters that roared between himself and the young girl and he soon stood beside her on the little patch of grass, secure and safe, under the rustling canopy of the ancient trees. Undine raised herself up a little and threw her arms round his neck, drawing him down to sit beside her on the soft ground of their leafy refuge. 'You can speak to me here, my handsome friend,' she whispered softly, 'that grumpy old pair cannot hear us here. And our leafy shelter is surely worth just as much as their miserable hut.'

'It is Heaven!' said Huldbrand and embraced the beautiful, affectionate young girl, kissing her passionately.

Meanwhile, the old fisherman had reached the bank of the stream and called over to the two young people, 'Hey, sir, I took you in as any honest man would have done and now you are carousing with my ward behind my back and what is more you leave me to wander around in the middle of the night worried half to death about her.'

'I have only just found her, sir,' the knight called back to him.

'Glad to hear it,' said the fisherman, 'now bring her across to me on dry land without delay.' Yet, once again Undine would not be told. She said that she would rather disappear for ever into the forest with the handsome stranger than return to the hut where no one did as she wished and which the handsome knight would sooner or later have to leave. She embraced Huldbrand and began to sing with indescribable sweetness:

'The stream left the misty valley,
Contentment to pursue.
Deep in the sea she found a home.
She will never return to you.'

The old fisherman wept bitterly as she sang, but this did not seem to affect her at all. She kissed and caressed her beloved, who was himself finally moved to speak, 'Undine, if the old man's tears do not trouble your heart, then they do mine. We must return to him.'

She looked up at him in amazement with her huge blue eyes and, after a pause, spoke slowly and hesitantly, 'If you think it is for the best, then so be it; I will do whatever you say. But the old man must first promise me that he will allow you to recount all that you saw in the woods without interruption and – oh, the rest will settle itself.'

'Come across, please, come across!' cried the old fisherman, unable to utter anything else. At the same time he stretched out his arms far over the water towards her and nodded to assure her that her wish would be granted, and, as he did so, the white hair fell around his face in a peculiar fashion, which reminded Huldbrand of the nodding white man in the forest. Determined not to be deterred by anything, however, the young knight took the beautiful girl in his arms and carried her over the torrent that rushed through the narrow channel between their tiny island and the safety of the bank. The old man embraced Undine and could hardly contain his joy; the old woman came too and embraced the returning girl heartily. There was no further thought of recrimination, the less so because Undine too, quite forgetting her contrary mood, almost overwhelmed her guardians with her sweetness and affection.

When they had all finally come to their senses after the joy of the reunion, day was just breaking over the lake, the storm had abated and the birds sang merrily in the wet branches. As Undine insisted on hearing the knight's tale as promised, the old couple happily acquiesced to her demands. Breakfast was laid out under the trees that stood behind the hut near the lake and Undine sat herself down in the grass at Huldbrand's feet, heartily pleased, for she wanted nothing more. Then the knight began his tale.

CHAPTER 4

What the Knight Had Encountered in the Forest

'Some eight days hence, I rode into the imperial city that lies beyond the forest. Shortly after my arrival, there was jousting and running at the ring and I spared neither steed nor lance in my enjoyment. I was resting in the stalls and was just handing my helmet to one of my knaves when a most beautiful woman caught my eye. She stood watching from a dais and was most magnificently clad. I inquired of my neighbour and discovered that the charming maiden was named Bertalda and that she was the ward of a powerful duke who resided in the area. I was aware that she was looking at me too and, as is often the case with us young knights, my steady horsemanship at once acquired a certain urgency. That evening at the ball I was Bertalda's companion and remained by her side for all eight days of the festivities –'

Huldbrand was interrupted by a smarting pain in his left hand, which hung down at his side, and his eyes were drawn to the painful spot. Undine had bitten into his finger with her pearl-white teeth and seemed quite sullen and angry. Suddenly, however, she looked at him wistfully with a tender expression and whispered very softly, 'You deserve it.' Then she hid her face and the knight, pensive and somewhat bemused, continued his tale:

'She is a proud and wayward maiden, this Bertalda. I did not like her nearly as much on the second day as I had done on the first, and on the third even less. Yet, I remained with her because she was nicer to me than she was to all the other knights, and so it happened too that in jest I asked for her glove as a favour. "Only if you, and you alone," she said, "can tell me what lies in the notorious forest." Her favour did not mean all that much to me but a promise is a promise and an honourable knight will not wait to be asked a second time to carry out such a task –'

'I think she was in love with you,' interrupted Undine.

'It seemed so,' replied Huldbrand.

'Well,' cried the girl aloud, 'she must be really rather stupid! To send away the one she loves! And, what is more, into a forest that is cursed. The wood and its secret could have waited for ever had I been in her shoes.'

'I set off yesterday morning,' continued the knight, smiling kindly at Undine. 'The trunks of the trees shone red and slender in the morning sun, which bathed the green grass in pure, bright light, and the leaves were whispering so merrily to one another that in my heart I had to laugh that anyone could expect anything untoward to happen in such a delightful place. "It should not take long to get through the forest, there and back," I said to myself, filled with light-hearted contentment. Before I knew it, however, I found myself deep among the green shadows with not the slightest visible trace of the plain behind me. All at once it struck me that I could quite easily become lost in the mighty forest and that this was perhaps the only danger to threaten the traveller there. I pulled up and looked around to pinpoint the position of the sun, which had, meanwhile, risen a little further. As I looked upwards, I saw a black object sitting in the branches of a tall oak tree. I first thought it was a bear and went for my blade; then it spoke to me in a voice that was human but quite harsh and ugly: "If it were not for me up here nibbling off the branches, what else would there be to roast you on at midnight, Mister White Nose?" And with that it grinned and rustled the branches so that my steed shied and bolted away with me before I had time to make out exactly what kind of devil's creature it was.'

'There is no need to mention his name,' said the old fisherman, crossing himself; his wife did the same.

Undine gazed at her beloved with shining eyes and said, 'The best of it is that they did not really roast you after all. Carry on, my handsome young friend.'

The knight continued his tale. 'I was almost dashed against the tree trunks and branches as I clung to my shying horse; it was dripping wet with fear and sweat and would not be made to stop. Eventually, it made straight for a stony chasm; all at once a tall white man seemed to thrust himself straight into the path of the crazed animal. The horse stopped in fright and it was only as I regained control that it became clear that my saviour was not in fact a white man but instead a shining silver stream, which had come cascading down the small hillside next to me, gushing violently across our path and barring my steed's way.'

'Thank you, dear stream!' cried Undine, clapping her hands. The old man, however, looked to the ground, deep in thought, and shook his head.

'I had barely settled myself in the saddle again and taken proper hold of the reins,' continued Huldbrand, 'when a strange little man appeared at my side. He was small and ugly beyond measure, yellow-brown in colour and with a nose that was not much smaller than the rest of his body. His wide muzzle of a mouth grinned with an air of bumbling courtesy and he scraped his feet and bowed before me a thousand times. Feeling that the whole farcical expedition had gone quite far enough, I thanked him briefly, turned my still quivering steed around and sought another adventure or, in the absence of one, the way home, for the sun had risen past midday during my mad chase and now sank towards the west; but the little chap sprang round with lightning speed and stood once more before my horse. "Out of my way!" I said angrily. "The animal is wild and could quite easily run you down." "Hey," growled the little man as he laughed even more horribly and stupidly, "give me some money first – after all, I stopped your horse; without me you would be lying down in that stony chasm, horse and all, eh!" "Please stop pulling those faces," I said, "and take your money, even if you are lying, for it was the lucky stream there that saved me, not you, you miserable imp." With that, I dropped a gold coin into the oddly fashioned cap that he held out towards me. Then I rode on; he called after me, moving with unbelievable speed, and before I knew it he was once more by my side. I spurred on my horse to a gallop and he galloped alongside me, even though it seemed to cause him some degree of pain and despite the strange, half-ridiculous, half-hideous contortions his body suffered in the process. He was holding the gold coin in the air and with each bound he cried: "False money! False coin! False coin! False money!" His hollow chest wheezed so much after every word that I was sure he was about to collapse dead on the ground, as his horrible red tongue hung right out of his gaping mouth. I pulled up, perturbed, and demanded an explanation. "What is all this shouting about? Take another gold coin, have another two but, please, leave me in peace." He launched once more into his hideous stream of civilities and growled, "Anything but gold, please, no gold, young sir; I have more than enough of that to be going on with; let me show you."

'All at once it was as if I could see right through the solid earth, as if it were made of green glass. The flat earth seemed as round as a ball and in it there were a great many goblins playing with silver and gold. They tumbled around head over heels, throwing the precious metal at each other in jest and blowing gold dust cheekily in each other's faces. My ugly companion stood half in and half out; he had the others hand him up a great pile of gold, showed it to me with a smile and then threw it fistful after fistful into the unknown depths of the chasm. Then he showed the goblins the gold coin that I had given him; they were beside themselves with laughter, hissing at me. In the end, they all stretched out their pointed metal-stained fingers towards me. The rabble grew wilder, denser and ever more frantic the closer it came; I was overcome by terror just as my horse had been before me. I spurred him on and chased off into the woods for a second time; I do not know how far.

'When I eventually came to a halt, the evening air around me was cool. Shining through the branches, I could see a white footpath, which I thought must lead through the forest back to the city. I wanted to make my way along it but a snow-white, almost indistinguishable, face with constantly changing features was looking out at me from behind the leaves; I tried to avoid him but he was there wherever I went. Infuriated, I finally decided to charge at him with my horse. A white foam sprayed up at myself and my horse, blinding us both and forcing us to turn; and so he drove us step by step further from the path, not allowing us to move freely in any direction except one. Once we had set off this way, then he remained close behind us but never did us the slightest harm. Every so often, when I turned round to look at him, I saw that the white foaming face sat on top of an equally white, quite gigantic, body. Yet, other times I thought it was a moving stream but I could never quite decide which. So horse and rider, both tired, gave in to the white man, who kept nodding at us as if he were saying, "That is right! That is right!" At length, we emerged here at the edge of the forest where I saw the grass and the water and your little hut and where the tall white man disappeared.'

'Thank goodness he has gone,' said the old fisherman and began to discuss how the guest could best make his way back to his own people in the city. Undine giggled secretively to herself.

Huldbrand noticed her smiling. 'I thought you were pleased to have me here; why are you so happy to hear talk of my leaving?' he asked.

'Because you cannot leave,' replied Undine. 'Go on, try to cross the flooded stream, in a boat, on horseback or alone, however you like. Or rather – do not try, for you would soon be smashed to pieces on the branches and stones that the water sweeps along with such lightning speed. And as for the lake, I know very well that father is not allowed far enough out in his boat.'

Huldbrand stood up smiling to see if what Undine said was true; the old man accompanied him and the girl skipped jovially alongside them. It was all exactly as Undine had said and the knight had no choice but to consent to staying on the peninsula-turned-island until the floods had subsided. As the three of them returned to the hut after their walk, the knight whispered in the young girl's ear: 'Well, what do you think, little Undine? Are you annoyed that I must stay?'

'I am not so sure,' she replied peevishly; 'if I had not bitten you, who knows what else you might have had to tell about Bertalda in your story!'

CHAPTER 5

How the Knight Lived on the Peninsula

You have perhaps, dear reader, at some time in the constant hustle and bustle of life, found a place where you were at ease; a place where the love of hearth, home and restful calm was once more kindled in your heart; a place where it seemed as if your homeland was adorned with all the many blooms of childhood; a place where a love both pure and sincere seemed to rise from the graves of the dear departed; a place where it felt right to live and to build. If you were perhaps misled in this and later painfully regretted the mistake is not our concern, and you will not be willing to upset yourself further with its bitter aftertaste. Still, if that indescribable feeling, that angelic sense of peace, were to rise in you anew, then you would have some notion of how Knight Huldbrand felt during his stay on the strip of land. He would often watch the stream flowing from the forest with a sense of heartfelt contentment as it grew in strength every day, widening its bed and further prolonging the isolation of the island. He would spend part of the day out stalking with an old crossbow he had found in a corner of the hut and had managed to repair. He hunted for birds and those he was able to catch were delivered to the kitchen to be roasted. Each time he returned with his catch, Undine would scold him relentlessly for having so wickedly taken the life of the poor delightful little animals who frequented the skies above the lake; indeed, she often cried bitterly at the sight of the dead creatures. Yet if he came home another time without having shot anything, then she would scold just as harshly, for his incompetence and carelessness meant they would now be forced to put up with fish and crabs. Her charming angry outbursts delighted him – all the more so for she usually sought to make up for her bad temper with the sweetest caresses. The old couple had come to accept the intimacy of the two youngsters; they seemed like an engaged or even a married couple who lived with them on the island, torn away from the mainland, in order to lend the support they needed in their old age. It was this very isolation that made young Huldbrand feel as if he were already Undine's groom. It was as if the world beyond the surrounding flood waters no longer existed; as if contact with other people across the water were an impossibility; and when, after a while, his steed whinnied at him, as if expressing the desire to return once more to chivalrous deeds, or the solemn gleam of the crest embroidered on his saddle and horse blanket caught his eye, or his magnificent sword fell unexpectedly from the nail upon which it hung in the hut and in falling slipped from the sheath – then he assuaged his doubts with the thought that Undine was in truth no fisherman's daughter but had in all probability been born of a noble foreign house of the highest rank. The one thing he truly could not bear was to hear the old woman scold Undine in his presence. Although the moody girl generally laughed it off quite openly, it seemed to him as if this were a slight on his honour, and yet he could not say the old fisherwoman was in the wrong for Undine usually deserved to be reproached at least ten times as often as she actually was. Thus he remained well-disposed in his heart towards the old woman and life continued in its quiet, comfortable way.

The peace was, however, soon to be shattered. The fisherman and the knight were in the habit of enjoying a jug of wine together with their midday meal or in the evening when the wind howled outside at nightfall. Now the entire supply, which the fisherman had brought with him little by little from the town, was at an end, and this had made the two men quite ill-tempered. Undine joked with them merrily the whole day long but they did not join in with their usual levity. Towards evening, she went out of the hut in order, she said, to get away from their two miserable long faces. When, at dusk, it looked likely to become stormy again and the water had already begun to howl and bubble, the knight and the fisherman ran anxiously from the door to fetch the girl home, their fear recalling the night when Huldbrand first came to the hut. Undine was, however, already on her way towards them, clapping her hands in glee. 'What will you give me if I get you some wine? Actually, you do not need to give me anything,' she continued, 'for I will be quite satisfied just to see you look a little happier and a little more enthusiastic than you have this last tedious day. Just come with me; the forest stream has washed up a barrel on the bank, and I would readily wager a whole week of sleep that it is a barrel of wine.' The men followed her and did indeed find a barrel floating in a sheltered inlet, which they hoped might contain the noble beverage they so desired. They rolled it into the hut as quickly as possible for, judging by the evening sky, the weather was about to worsen and even in the half light the white crests of the waves on the lake could already be seen foaming upwards as if in search of the rain that was about to fall. Undine helped them as best she could and, as the rain began to pour down on them, turned to threaten the heavy clouds in jest. 'Hey you! Take care not to soak us! We are not nearly under cover yet.' The old man condemned this as sinful presumptuousness but she merely chuckled to herself and no one was any the worse for it. Indeed, contrary to expectation, all three were still dry when they reached the comfort of the hearth with their catch, and only after the barrel had been opened and discovered to contain a most palatable wine did the clouds burst open with pouring rain as the storm thundered through the tree-tops and over the angry waves of the lake.

They soon succeeded in filling a few bottles from the great barrel, which would last for many days, and they sat drinking and joking together, safe and cosy by the glow of the hearth as the wild storm raged outside. Then the old fisherman suddenly became quite serious and said, 'Oh dear God, here we are enjoying this noble gift and yet whoever once owned it, who had it stolen from him by the torrent, probably lost his life for it.'

'That need not be so!' declared Undine, filling the knight's glass with a smile.

'I swear by my honour, dear sir,' Huldbrand proclaimed, 'that if I knew how to find and rescue him then there is no journey into darkness nor any danger that would hold me back. This much I can assure you: if I ever find my way back to more inhabited lands then I will seek him out, or his heirs, and replace this wine two- and threefold.' This pleased the old man; he nodded at the knight approvingly and then emptied his glass contentedly, his conscience eased.

Undine turned to Huldbrand and said, 'You may do as you wish with all your talk of recompense and your gold, but as for chasing after him and seeking him out – such nonsense. I would cry my eyes out if you were to be lost while doing such a thing, and, anyway, surely you would rather stay here with me and a glass of good wine?'

'But of course,' replied Huldbrand, laughing.

'So,' said Undine, 'you were talking nonsense. For charity begins at home, and what do other people matter to us?'

The old woman turned away from her, sighing and shaking her head; the fisherman, however, quite forgot his customary indulgence towards the delicate young girl and rebuked her sharply. 'It sounds as if you had been raised by heathens and Turks,' he concluded. 'May God forgive us both, you spoiled little child.'

'Well, that is how I feel,' replied Undine; 'it makes no difference who raised me or what you say.'

'Enough!' barked the fisherman, and Undine, who, for all her impudence, was actually quite easily alarmed, took fright and, quivering, sidled up to Huldbrand and asked him very quietly:

'Are you angry too, my handsome friend?' The knight squeezed her soft hand and stroked her curls. His anger at the old man's severity prevented him from saying another word and so, filled with both anger and shame, the two couples sat opposite each other in silence.

CHAPTER 6

A Wedding

The silence was broken by a soft knocking at the door, which startled them all. Such insignificant but unexpected events are sometimes the cause of great excitement, but in this case even more so for the cursed forest lay near by and the strip of land was inaccessible to human visitors. As they looked at each other nervously, the knocking sound could be heard once more, this time accompanied by a deep groaning. The knight went for his sword, to which the old man responded quietly, 'If it is that which I fear, then no weapon can help us.'

Meanwhile, Undine had gone towards the door and begun to shout angrily and impudently, 'If you are here to cause trouble, spirits of the earth, then Kühleborn shall find you something better to do.' These strange words served only to frighten the others even more and they looked at the girl with increased apprehension. Huldbrand was about to ask her a question when a voice came from outside:

'I am no spirit of the earth, merely a spirit who still resides in an earthly body. If you want to help me and live in fear of God, you there in the hut, then open the door.' On hearing these words, Undine opened the door and shone a lantern out into the stormy night. There stood an old priest, who was quite taken aback at the unexpected sight of the beautiful girl. He must have thought there were spirits and magic at work for him to behold such a lovely vision in the doorway of such a miserable hut.

He began to pray: 'Heavenly spirits, praise the lord God!'

'I am not a ghost,' said Undine smiling, 'or am I really so ugly? Anyway, surely you can see that such pious words do not frighten me. I know all about God and how to praise him – each in their own way, of course; that is why he made us. Come inside, honourable father, you are among good people.'

The clergyman entered, bowing as he looked around him. He seemed most amiable and worthy. Water was dripping from every fold of his dark robes, from his long white beard and from the white hair on his head. The fisherman and the knight led him into a room and gave him some other clothes while they handed the priest's robes to the women in the main room to dry. The strange old man thanked them most humbly and kindly but firmly refused to put on the knight's shining cloak, which they first handed him to wear; he chose instead an old grey smock belonging to the fisherman. As they came back into the room, the housewife immediately offered her great chair to the priest and would not rest until he had settled in it, 'For,' she said, 'you are old and exhausted and a clergyman to boot.' Undine pushed the little stool, upon which she usually sat beside Huldbrand, under the feet of the stranger and proved to be quite polite and charming in taking care of the old man. Huldbrand whispered in her ear, teasing her about it, but she answered him most earnestly:

'He is in the service of the One who made us all; that is not to be taken lightly.' The knight and the fisherman then refreshed the priest with food and wine and once he had recovered a little he began to explain how, the day before, he had left his monastery, which lay far away across the great lake, in order to travel to the seat of the bishop. His task was to report the suffering that the current unexpected floods had caused both the monastery and its surrounding villages. That day, towards evening, having already taken a long and roundabout route to avoid these very floods, he had been forced to cross a flooded inlet with the help of two trusty ferrymen. 'Hardly had our little boat touched the waves,' he continued, 'than a terrible storm broke. Indeed, it still rages above our heads now. It was as if the waters had lain in wait for us and now sought to swirl us round in a frantic dance. The oars were soon torn from my boatmen's hands and smashed to pieces as they were swept away from us by waves. As for ourselves, we were tossed around helplessly on the surging waters, quite at the mercy of the unheeding forces of Nature, until we reached your distant shore, which came rising into view through the mist and spray. Then the little boat began to spin round even more wildly; I do not know whether it capsized or whether I fell out. I was driven onwards in dread of the terrible death that awaited me, until a wave washed me up under the trees on your island here.'

'Indeed. An island!' exclaimed the fisherman. 'Not so long ago it was just a strip of land but ever since the forest stream and the lake have become afflicted with this madness, we find ourselves in a quite different situation.'

'I thought as much as I crept along the shore in the darkness,' said the priest. 'Unable to make out anything but the wild thundering around me, I finally caught sight of a worn footpath, which seemed to disappear into the mêlée. Then I saw the light in your hut and ventured my way here, whereby I cannot thank my heavenly Father enough that, after saving me from the water, he led me to such pious people as yourselves, and all the more so for I cannot tell whether I shall ever see any people in this life again other than you four.'

'What do you mean by that?' asked the fisherman.

'Do you know how long this upheaval of the elements is set to last?' asked the clergyman. 'For I am advanced in years and the river of my life is quite likely to have dried up under the earth long before the flood waters of the stream subside. And, anyway, it would not be impossible for even more raging water to force its way between yourselves and that forest over there until you have been torn so far from the rest of the land that your little fishing boats can no longer reach the other side and for the inhabitants on the mainland, preoccupied by their own concerns, to forget all about you in your old age.'

Frightened by this prospect, the old woman crossed herself and said, 'God forbid!'

The fisherman looked at her, laughing, and said, 'How strange people are! It would make no difference at all, at least not to you. Tell me, have you ever ventured any further than the edge of the forest these many years? Have you seen any people other than Undine and myself? It is only recently that the knight and the priest have joined us and they would have to stay with us if we became a forgotten island, so you would, in fact, have more company than before.'

'I am not sure,' said the old woman, 'it is a very strange feeling to think that you are to be separated from other people for ever, even if you would not normally see them.'

'Stay with us, stay with us!' whispered Undine very softly, half singing, and nestled even further into Huldbrand's side, but he was deep in thought. On hearing the priest's words, the world beyond the stream seemed to drift even further into the darkness, whereas the lush island on which he now lived became greener and seemed to smile upon his soul with renewed vitality. There was the blushing bride, as fair as the most beautiful rose on the little strip of land, in the whole world even; there was the priest readily to hand; and there was the angry look that the old woman gave the beautiful girl for leaning too close to her beloved in the presence of the clergyman; a look which, it seemed, was about to be followed by a reproachful tirade. The words fell from the knight's lips as he turned towards the priest:

'You see a bridal couple before you, honourable sir, and if this girl and these worthy old fisherfolk have nothing against it, then you shall marry us this very evening.'

The old couple were utterly amazed. They had, of course, often thought of such a thing but never actually discussed it and now, as the knight spoke, it seemed like something quite new and unexpected. Undine had suddenly become quite serious and stared thoughtfully at the ground before her, while the priest inquired as to the exact circumstances and asked for the agreement of the old couple. After much discussion, they came to an accord; the old woman went to prepare the bridal chamber for the young couple and to look out two sacred candles, which she had kept for a long time and which would be suited for use at the marriage ceremony. Meanwhile, the knight fumbled with his golden chain and tried to detach two gold rings for exchange with the bride. When she spotted this, Undine was torn from her thoughts and exclaimed, 'No, not like that! My parents did not send me into this world a beggar woman; what is more, they must have known long ago that there would be an evening such as this.' With that she hurried out of the door and returned immediately with two magnificent rings. One she gave to her groom, the other she kept for herself. The old fisherman was quite amazed by this; his wife, who had just returned, even more so, for they had never seen the child with these jewels before. 'My parents had these little trinkets sewn into the very dress I happened to be wearing when I came to you,' explained Undine. 'They forbade me to ever mention them to anyone until the eve of my wedding. So I secretly removed them and kept them hidden until today.' The priest interrupted the ensuing questions and wonderment by lighting the sacred candles. He placed them on the table and asked the couple to stand opposite him. He then performed the brief ceremony, the old couple blessed the youngsters and the bride leaned thoughtfully upon the knight, trembling silently.

Then all at once the priest said, 'You are indeed odd people! I thought you said you were the only people on the island? Yet the whole way through the ceremony I could see a tall, handsome man in a white cloak looking in at the window opposite me. He must still be outside if you want to ask him in.'

'God save us!' gasped the old woman in fright. The old fisherman shook his head silently and Huldbrand leapt towards the window. He thought he just caught a glimpse of a white streak, which soon disappeared altogether in the darkness. He convinced the priest that he must have been mistaken and they settled down together companionably around the hearth.

CHAPTER 7

What Else Happened on the Wedding Night

Undine had been well-behaved and calm both before and during the wedding ceremony, but now it seemed as if all the strange whims and notions within her were set to resurface with added impudence. She invented all manner of childish tricks to tease her groom, her guardians, and even the priest, who had so recently been treated with such reverence. When the old woman attempted to protest, she was silenced by a few grave words from the knight, who grandly proclaimed Undine to be his wife. All the same, the knight himself was not particularly pleased with Undine's childish capers; but all his hints, coughs and rebukes were in vain. Granted, whenever the bride noticed her lover's displeasure – which happened a number of times – she would settle down a little and sit next to him, stroking his hair and whispering in his ear with a smile, all of which helped to smooth his increasingly furrowed brow. Yet, the very next moment, she would tear off once more on some wild whim and suddenly it was all far worse than before. At length the priest said, very seriously and very kindly, 'My dear child, one cannot look at you without being captivated, but take care from time to time to attune your soul, so that it is in harmony with that of your husband.'

'Soul!' Undine laughed at him. 'That sounds awfully nice and no doubt for the majority of people it is an edifying and useful rule to follow. But what if one has no soul, I ask you, what is there to bring into tune then? So it is for me.' The priest was silent and deeply wounded. He turned away from the girl with a melancholy expression. She, however, sidled up to him and said, 'Just hear me out and do not look so angry, for it pains me to see such anger on your face and it is wrong to hurt a creature who has done you no harm. Be patient with me and I will explain properly what I mean.'

They could see she was preparing to tell them something of great significance but all at once she hesitated and burst into a stream of miserable tears, as if overcome by some inner fear. None of those present knew quite what to make of her any more and they stared at her in silence with varying degrees of concern. Then, eventually drying her tears, she looked earnestly at the priest and said, 'It must be wonderful to have a soul, but at the same time it must be a terrible thing to bear. I ask, in the Lord's name, would it not be better never to have had one at all?' She fell silent again as if awaiting an answer. Her tears had stopped. They all rose from their seats and moved away from her, trembling as they did so, but she seemed only to have eyes for the clergyman. Her features had a look of fearful curiosity, which itself seemed quite terrible to the others. 'The soul must bear a terrible burden,' she continued when no one answered her. 'Most terrible! For even as it approaches, it overshadows me with such fear and sadness. Oh, I was so free, so happy before!' And she burst once more into tears and hid her face in the folds of her veil. The priest walked towards her with a serious expression and spoke to her, beseeching her in the name of the Lord to cast off her veil if any evil spirits possessed her. She sank to her knees before him, repeating every pious word he uttered, praising God and assuring him that she truly meant well with the world.

Finally, the priest turned to the knight and said, 'Sir, I now leave you alone with the woman you have married. As far as I can tell there is no evil in her but much that is strange. I recommend caution, love and loyalty.' With that he departed, followed by the fisherfolk who crossed themselves as they left.

Undine had fallen to her knees; she uncovered her face and, looking round timidly at Huldbrand, said, 'Oh, you will surely deny me now; yet I have done nothing wrong, poor, poor child that I am!' So delightful and touching were her words that all thoughts of horror and consternation vanished from the groom's mind. He rushed over and lifted her up in his arms. As she smiled through her tears, it was as if the morning light were shining playfully on tiny rivulets. 'You cannot keep away from me!' she whispered softly and confidently, stroking the knight's cheek with her soft little hand as she did so. He then banished the terrible thoughts that still lurked at the back of his mind and sought to convince him that he was betrothed to a fairy or some other evil, mocking creature from the spirit world; yet one question slipped out almost unintentionally:

'Dear Undine, tell me one thing, what was that you were saying about earth spirits when the priest knocked on the door, and about Kühleborn?'

'Fairy tales! Children's fairy tales!' said Undine, laughing once more with her accustomed gaiety. 'In the beginning I frightened you with it, and in the end you frightened me. So ends the song and the whole wedding night.'

'Indeed it does not,' said the knight, quite overcome with his love for Undine. He blew out the candles and, bathed in the moonlight that shone brightly through the window, carried his beloved beauty to the bridal chamber, covering her in a thousand kisses as he did so.

CHAPTER 8

The Day after the Wedding

The fresh light of morning awoke the young couple. Undine hid herself bashfully under the covers and Huldbrand lay quietly beside her, lost in his own thoughts. During the night, each time he had succeeded in falling asleep, he had been disturbed by strange and gruesome dreams of grinning, furtive phantoms who sought to disguise themselves as beautiful women and whose faces would, all at once, turn into those of dragons; and each time, when he awoke, startled from his slumbers by these horrible images, the pale, cold moonlight was still shining outside the window. He looked in horror at Undine, on whose breast he had fallen asleep and who slept, her grace and beauty unchanged, beside him. Then he lightly kissed her rosy lips and fell asleep once more, only to be awoken again in terror. Once he had considered it all rationally in the clear morning light, he reproached himself for having entertained such doubts, which might have led him to misjudge his beautiful wife. He openly begged her forgiveness. She sighed deeply as she gave him her delicate hand but remained silent. Still, an intense and heartfelt look in her eyes, the like of which he had not seen before, left him in no doubt that Undine bore him no ill. Cheered by this, he dressed and went to join the others. The three of them sat round the hearth with concerned faces but without daring to say a word. It looked as if the priest was engaged in silent prayer in order to avert any possible evil. Yet, the sight of the young husband in such good spirits soon smoothed their furrowed brows; indeed, the old fisherman began to jest with the knight in a quite amiable manner, which even brought a smile to the old woman's face. At length, Undine was ready and made her appearance; they all stood to greet her, yet remained where they were in amazement, for although the young woman still seemed so familiar, she was somehow quite altered. The priest was the first to approach her, fatherly affection in his shining eyes. As he raised his hand in blessing, the beautiful woman sank to her knees before him, trembling with reverence. With a few humble words she begged his forgiveness for the foolish things she might have said the day before and, in a touching voice, asked him to pray for the good of her soul. Then she stood up, kissed her guardians and thanked them for all they had done for her. 'Oh, now I feel it from the bottom of my heart, how much, how so very much, you have done for me, you dear, dear people!' At first she could barely tear herself away from their embraces, but no sooner had she noticed that the old woman was concerned with preparing breakfast than she stood herself at the stove, declaring that the old woman was not to strain herself in any way.

So she remained the whole day long: calm, friendly and attentive, both housewife and tender, bashful child. The three who had known her for some time expected some strange change in her mood at any moment, but they waited in vain. Undine remained angelic and tender. The priest could hardly take his eyes from her and said several times to her groom, 'Yesterday, sir, by my unworthy hand, the grace of Heaven saw fit to bless you with a treasure; guard it well and it shall bring you salvation, now and for ever.'

As evening came Undine hung upon the knight's arm with humble affection and led him gently out of the door where the setting sun shone softly over the fresh grass and around the slender trunks of the trees. The young woman's eyes swam as if filled with a dew of melancholy and love; a tender, anxious secret seemed to hover on her lips, which could only be heard in barely audible sighs. Silently she led her lover further; anything he said was met merely with a look, which gave no direct answer to his question but which revealed a whole Heaven of love and timid devotion. Presently they reached the bank of the flooded forest stream and the knight was amazed to see its waves becalmed as it seeped away to a trickle with no sign of its recent savagery and spate. 'By tomorrow it will have dried up completely,' said the beautiful woman, tearfully, 'and you may travel wherever you like without hindrance.'

'Not without you, Undine,' replied the knight, laughing. 'Anyway, even if I did want to run off, then church and clergy, emperor and empire would all be at my heels to return the fugitive to you.'

'It is for you to choose,' whispered the young girl, half crying, half smiling. 'Although, I think perhaps you do truly want me; I am too dear to your heart. Carry me across to the little island that lies before us. You must make your decision there. I could easily slip under the waves but it is so comfortable in your arms and if you cast me away then at least I will have lain in them one last time.' Huldbrand was filled with a strange sense of apprehension and emotion and was unsure what to reply. He took her in his arms and carried her across, only now realizing that it was the same small island from which he had carried her back to the fisherman on that first night. Once across, he laid her down in the soft grass and was about to cuddle up to his beautiful burden when she said, 'No, over there, opposite me. I want to be able to see into your eyes before I hear your lips speak. Listen carefully to what I have to tell you.' And she began:

'You should know, my love, that there are living creatures among the elements that look quite like mortals but are seldom seen by them. Wondrous salamanders glitter and play in the flames, withered, bad-tempered gnomes live deep in the earth; treefolk who belong to the air inhabit the forests; a multitude of water spirits reside in the lakes and rivers and streams. They have a wonderful life in their ringing crystal vaults with the sky looking in, bright with sun and stars; tall trees of coral, heavy with blue and crimson fruits, are aglow in their gardens; they wander over pure sea sand and beautifully coloured shells and amid the many treasures of the old world – those which the new is not worthy to behold – that have been covered over by the secret silver veils of the tides. There are noble monuments, resplendent, tall and grave, sprinkled with dew by the caressing waters that tempt forth beautiful marsh flowers and garlands of reeds. Those who live there are quite charming and lovely to look at, more so mostly than people are. Many a fisherman has been lucky enough to overhear a mermaid as she rose above the tide to sing. The creatures' beauty became known far and wide and the people gave them the name Undines. And, indeed, you have a true Undine before you now, dear friend.'

The knight tried to convince himself that his beautiful wife had fallen into one of her strange moods and that she was having fun teasing him with wild imagined tales. Yet, no matter how hard he tried to convince himself of this, he could not for one moment believe that her words were anything other than the truth; a strange shiver ran down his spine; he stared intently at the lovely narrator, unable to utter a single word. She shook her head sadly, sighed deeply, and then continued:

'We ought to be far better off than you other human beings – we see ourselves as human beings too, for we are alike in mind and body – but there is one quite awful thing you must know. We and those like us in the other elements simply vanish and fade in spirit and body so that not a trace of us remains and, whereas you mortals eventually awake to a purer life, we must stay behind, where sand and spark and wind and wave remain. And so we have no souls; the element moves us and often does our bidding as long as we live, yet it turns us to dust as soon as we die. Still, we are happy and never complain, just like the nightingales and little goldfish and other pretty children of Nature too. But surely we all want more than we have been given. Such was the case with my father who is a powerful water duke in the Mediterranean Sea. His only daughter was to be blessed with a soul, even if she would then suffer the many pains of those who have one. Our kind can, however, gain a soul only through the blessed union of love with one of your kind, and so I now have a soul. I thank you for it, my beloved, and I will still thank you for it even if you make my life an utter misery, for what will become of me if you refuse me now and cast me away? Still, I would not wish to be kept by deception, and if you wish to cast me away, then do it now; return to the bank alone. I will dive into this stream, who is my uncle and who lives his strange life as a hermit here in the forest, far from his other friends. Yet he is powerful and worth more than many great rivers put together. Just as he brought me here to the fisherfolk as a tiny laughing child, so he will also take me home to my parents, a loving, suffering woman with a soul.'

She wanted to say more but Huldbrand took hold of her and carried her back to the bank, deeply moved and overwhelmed with love. Only then did he swear amid tears and kisses never to leave his lovely wife and proclaimed himself happier than the Greek sculptor Pygmalion whose beautiful statue had been brought to life by Venus to become his beloved. Undine walked back to the hut with his arms around her and now felt sure in her heart that she could never regret leaving the glass palace of her strange father.

CHAPTER 9

How the Knight Took His Young Bride with Him

The next morning as Huldbrand awoke, his beautiful companion was not at his side and he began again to entertain the strange thoughts that suggested his marriage and the charming Undine herself were nothing but a passing apparition or a trick. Just then she entered the room, kissed him, sat on the bed beside him and said, 'I went out early to see if my uncle has kept his word. He has already guided all the flood waters back to his own calm channel and now he flows, as he did before, in pensive solitude through the forest glades. His friends in the water and air are also at peace; everything will be calm again as it should be in these parts and you can travel home as soon as you like without getting your feet wet.' Although wide awake, Huldbrand was unable to come to terms with his wife's strange kin and felt as if he were still dreaming. Yet, he masked his concern and his lovely wife's endless charm soon laid any sense of foreboding to rest.

When, a little later, he stood at the door and looked out over the grassy strip of land with its clear watery borders, he felt so at ease in this, the cradle of his love, that he said, 'Why should we travel today? We shall surely not find better times out there in the world than those we have had in this secret refuge. Let us watch the sun go down here two or three times more.'

'As my lord wishes,' replied Undine with kind humility. 'It is just that the old people must already suffer greatly in parting from me and if they were then to sense the true soul in me and see how I am able to love and honour from the heart then their poor eyes would not be able to bear the weight of so many tears. They still think that my calm and devotion are nothing more than they were wont to expect from me – like the calm waters of the lake when the air is still. They still think that they might be just as able to befriend a little tree or flower as they will me. Do not make me reveal this newly received gift of love to them in the very moment when it shall be lost to them for ever. And how could I hide it from them if we were to remain here together any longer?'

Huldbrand saw she was right; he went to the old couple and discussed with them the journey that was to begin within the hour. The priest offered to accompany the young couple and after a brief farewell he and the knight lifted the beautiful woman on to the horse and walked with her quickly towards the forest over the dried-up bed of the stream. Undine cried silent but bitter tears, the old people wailed aloud after her. It seemed that they did have some inkling of what they were losing in their lovely foster-daughter.

The three travellers had reached the darkest shadows of the forest in silence. It must have been a pleasant sight in the leafy grove to see the beautiful woman on the nobly adorned horse, watchfully accompanied on one side by the honoured priest in his white robes, on the other by the handsome young knight in colourful, bright clothing with his magnificent sword. Huldbrand had eyes only for his lovely wife; Undine, who had dried her precious tears, had eyes only for him, and they soon fell into a silent exchange of looks and gestures from which they were distracted only much later by the sound of lowered voices as the priest conversed with a fourth travelling companion who had joined them unnoticed.

He wore a white tunic not unlike the priest's robes except that his hood was pulled down over his face and the whole garment swirled in folds around him so much that he was forever having to gather it up and throw it over his arm or effect some other re-arrangement, yet without it ever seeming to hinder his gait. When the young couple became aware of him, he was just saying, 'And so I have lived for many years in these woods, honourable sir, but not in such a way that you could call me a hermit, not in your sense of the word. For, as I said, I know nothing of penance and do not believe myself to be particularly in need of it. I love the wood simply because it has its own very special beauty. I do enjoy wandering through the dark shadows and foliage in my flowing white robes and occasionally a sweet ray of sunshine shines down on me quite unexpectedly.'

'You are a most remarkable man,' replied the priest, 'and I would like to know more about you.'

'And who might you be, then, to change the subject?'

'They call me Father Heilmann,' said the clergyman, 'and I come from the abbey of Mariagruss on the other side of the lake.'

'I see,' replied the stranger. 'My name is Kühleborn and, if we want to be polite, one might just as well call me by the title Sir Kühleborn. I am as free as the birds in the trees and most likely even a little more. Indeed, I now have something to tell that young woman over there.' And before they knew it, he was at the priest's other side, close by Undine, stretching up high to whisper something in her ear.

She turned away in fright, saying, 'I will have nothing more to do with you.'

'Well, well,' laughed the stranger, 'what a terribly good match you must have made for yourself if you can afford to renounce your kin. Have you forgotten your Uncle Kühleborn who so loyally carried you here on his back?'

'I beg of you,' replied Undine, 'not to show your face to me again. I am afraid of you now; and what if my husband should learn to fear me when he sees me in the company of such strange kith and kin?'

'My dear niece,' said Kühleborn, 'you must not forget that I am here to guide you; the ghostly earth spirits might play silly tricks on you otherwise. Just let me walk along beside you quietly; by the way, the old priest over there remembers me better than you seem to, for he assured me before that I was very familiar to him and that I must have been in the little boat from which he fell into the water. It was me, of course, for I was indeed the very spout of water which tore him from it and swept him up afterwards on to dry land, safe and sound in time for your betrothal.'

Undine and the knight looked at Father Heilmann but he seemed to be wandering on lost in a dream, quite unaware of everything that was being said. Then Undine said to Kühleborn, 'I see the edge of the forest over there already. We no longer require your help and nothing alarms us more than your presence. So I beg you, with love and goodwill, please be gone and leave us to travel on in peace.' This seemed to anger Kühleborn. He pulled an ugly face and leered at Undine, who screamed loudly and called to her husband for help. The knight rounded the horse in a flash and swiped at Kühleborn's head with his sharp blade, but he found himself hacking at a waterfall, which tumbled from a high cliff next to them and which drenched them suddenly with a splashing noise that sounded almost like laughter.

Then the priest spoke, as if suddenly awoken from a dream: 'I have long been expecting something of the sort, for the stream seemed to run so close to the ridge above us. At first I even thought it resembled a man who might speak at any moment.'

As the waterfall crashed down the cliff, it roared in Huldbrand's ear: 'Swift knight, sturdy knight, I am not angered, I shall not quarrel; just guard your charming little wife well, oh sturdy knight, oh swift young knight!'

A few steps further and they were out in the open. The imperial city lay gleaming before them and the evening sun, which bathed its towers in gold, obligingly dried the clothes of the drenched travellers.

CHAPTER 10

How They Lived in the City

The sudden disappearance of the young Knight Huldbrand von Ringstetten had caused a great upset in the imperial city. There was much concern among the people, who had all become quite fond of him, in part because of his skill at the tournament and at the ball, but also because of his mild manner and friendly demeanour. His servants did not wish to leave the city without their master, not that any of them had found the courage to follow him into the shadows of the fearsome forest. So they remained in their lodgings, hoping idly, as people tend to do, and keeping the memory of the missing master alive with their wailing and moaning. When, soon after, the great storms and floods became ever more fierce, people were increasingly convinced of the certain demise of the handsome stranger. Bertalda too mourned quite openly and cursed herself for having enticed him to undertake the wretched ride into the forest. Her noble guardians had come to collect her but Bertalda begged them to stay on with her until it was known for certain whether Huldbrand was alive or dead.

She tried to persuade the various young knights who courted her ardently to follow the noble adventurer into the forest, but she refused to promise her hand in return for such a dare, for she still hoped to win the heart of the returning knight, and a glove or a ribbon, even a kiss, was not enough reward to risk life and limb in order to bring back such a dangerous rival.

So when Huldbrand reappeared so unexpectedly, the servants, the townspeople, indeed, almost everyone, were delighted, except for Bertalda. For if the others were pleased to see him return with such a beautiful wife and Father Heilmann, the witness of their wedding, Bertalda could do no more than be miserable about it. For she had truly come to love the young knight with all her heart and her sadness at his absence had made this far more widely known among the people than she would perhaps have wished. Nevertheless, she kept her wits about her, put up with circumstances as they were and lived most amicably alongside Undine, whom everyone believed to be a princess, freed by Huldbrand from some evil spell in the forest. When she or her husband were asked about it, they managed to keep silent or find some clever response. Father Heilmann's lips were sealed for he suffered no idle gossip and, anyway, he had made his way back to the abbey soon after Huldbrand's return. And so the people were left to their own strange speculations and even Bertalda knew no more of the truth than anyone else.

Undine became fonder of the charming maiden with every passing day. 'We must have met each other somewhere before,' she would often say, 'or there must be some kind of strange connection between us, for without such a reason – you understand – without there being some deep, secret reason, one surely does not grow as fond of another from the first moment as I did of you.' And, indeed, Bertalda could not deny that she too felt a pull of familiarity and love towards Undine, despite having undoubted grounds for the bitterest complaint against her happy rival. Through this mutual affection, they both managed to further postpone the day of departure, one persuading the guardians, the other the husband; there was even talk that Bertalda should visit Undine for a while at Castle Ringstetten at the source of the Danube.

They were talking of just such a visit one evening as they wandered by starlight around the tree-ringed market-place of the imperial city. The young couple had collected Bertalda late in the evening to go for a walk and the three wandered companionably up and down under the deep blue sky. Their conversation was often interrupted by the need to admire the ornate fountain in the centre of the square and wonder at the strange rushing and bubbling sound, which soothed them, putting them in the best of spirits. The flickering of lights from the nearby houses stole through the shadows of the trees as the quiet chatter of capering children and other strollers drifted by. Alone but yet secure, enveloped in this lively, happy world, everything that had seemed difficult during the day seemed to resolve itself quite simply in the evening air. The three friends could no longer comprehend how Bertalda's travelling with them could be a cause of the slightest concern. Then, just as they were about to set a date for their departure together, a tall man approached them from the middle of the square, bowed respectfully and said something in Undine's ear. Annoyed at being disturbed by this trouble-maker, she drew the stranger to one side and they began to whisper with one another in what seemed to be a foreign tongue. Huldbrand thought he recognized the strange man and was staring at him so intently that he neither heard nor answered Bertalda's bemused questions. All at once Undine laughed and clapped her hands with joy. She quickly left the stranger, who shook his head gravely before retreating hastily and vanishing into the fountain. Huldbrand now thought he knew what was going on; Bertalda, however, asked, 'What did the master of the fountain want with you, dear Undine?'

The young woman laughed to herself mysteriously and replied, 'You will find out the day after tomorrow – on your name-day, my dear child.' And she would reveal nothing more. She invited Bertalda and her guardians to lunch on the appointed day and soon after they went their separate ways.

'Kühleborn?' Huldbrand asked his wife with a secret shiver, after they had taken leave of Bertalda and were walking through the darkening streets towards home.

'Yes, it was he,' answered Undine, 'and he wanted to bother me with all manner of stupid things! But in the middle of it all, quite contrary to his intentions, he brought me some most welcome news. If you wish to know this now, my dear lord and master, then you need only ask and I will open my heart to you. If, however, you want to do your Undine a great, great favour then you will wait until the day after tomorrow and share in the surprise.'

The knight gladly granted his wife what she so charmingly requested and, even as she fell asleep, she whispered to herself, 'How she will rejoice to hear what the master of the fountain had to say. Dear, dear Bertalda.'

CHAPTER 11

The Celebration of Bertalda's Name-day

The company had gathered round the table. Bertalda sat between Undine and Huldbrand, adorned like a spring goddess with jewels and flowers, the countless gifts of her guardians and friends. In keeping with time-honoured German tradition, at the end of the delicious meal the doors to the hall remained open as the dessert was served so that the people could look on and take pleasure in the merriment of the lords and ladies. Servants handed around wine and cakes to the watching crowd. Huldbrand and Bertalda waited with secret impatience for the promised explanation and as far as possible kept their eyes firmly fixed upon Undine. Yet the beautiful young woman maintained her silence and smiled secretly and happily to herself. Those who knew of her promise could see that she was bursting with the desire to reveal her much-anticipated secret and yet was holding it back with greedy denial just as children often do with their favourite treats. Bertalda and Huldbrand shared this sweet feeling, awaiting with hopeful apprehension the new joy that would soon be delivered to them from their friend's lips. Some among the company asked Undine to sing. The request seemed to come at just the right time. She had her lute brought straight away and began to sing:

'So bright is the day,
The flowers so gay,
Lofty grasses so sweet
On the lakeside do greet!
What shines there so brightly,
Twixt blades swaying lightly?
Is it a blossom, so white and dear,
Fallen from Heaven to bless us here?
But look, it is a child so fair! –
At play in the flowers, quite unaware,
Reaching to grasp each golden ray; –
From whence do you come this happy day?
Borne from a far and distant land
The waters cast you upon the sand; –
Dear child, there is no need to reach
With your tiny hand outstretched;
There is no hand to return your own.
But for the flowers, you are alone.
The secret of beauty is known to them,
To win a heart with a perfumed stem,
Yet here there is no comforting face,
Far from a mother's loving embrace.
Far too young to face life alone,
Your smiling lips still heaven's own,
For you, poor child, the best is gone,
Yet you know not what has been done.
But, see, a noble duke comes riding by
And halts his steed just where you lie;
A daughter schooled in noble ways
In his castle you spend your days.
You gained so much from his guiding hand,
And became the fairest in all the land,
But oh! the sweetest thing by far
Was left behind on that unknown shore.'

Undine laid down her lute with a wistful smile; the eyes of Bertalda's noble guardians were full of tears. 'That is just what happened the morning I found you, you poor, lovely orphan,' said the duke, deeply moved; 'this beautiful songstress is no doubt right; we were never able to give you the best.'

'We must also hear how the parents fared,' said Undine and, plucking the strings once more, she sang:

> 'Through empty rooms the mother goes,
> Clutter and chattels cast asunder in woe.
> She knows not what she seeks in her pain,
> But finds nothing there – emptiness reigns.

> 'Empty house! What pain words bring
> Once the home of the dearest thing,
> Tenderly nurtured by the light of day,
> Each night in a cradle she peacefully lay.

> 'The beeches are turning to green once more,
> The rays of the sun shine in at the door.
> But mother, your search must end in vain,
> Your dear one can never be with you again.

> 'And when the evening breezes blow,
> Father returns to the hearth's warm glow,
> At first as it moves him, a smile appears,
> But this joy will soon be followed by tears.

> 'Full well he knows that in each room,
> He shall find naught but deathly gloom,
> Nothing to hear but the mother's lament,
> No laughing child, once Heaven sent.'

'Oh, for God's sake, Undine, where are my parents?' cried Bertalda in tears. 'You know exactly, you have found out, you wondrous woman, for otherwise you would not have torn at my heart like this. Are they already here? Could it be?' Her eyes cast round the glittering assembly and rested for a while on a noble ruler's wife who sat next to her guardian. Undine turned back towards the door, her eyes brimming with the sweetest emotion.

'Where are the poor, waiting parents then?' she asked, and the old fisherman and his wife staggered from the watching crowd. They looked questioningly, first at Undine, then at the beautiful young woman who was said to be their daughter. 'It is she!' stammered the delighted messenger and the two old people flung their arms round the neck of their long-lost daughter, crying loudly and praising God.

Bertalda, however, tore herself free from their embraces in shock and anger. It was too much for her proud nature to have to bear such a reunion when she had been quite convinced that her previous splendour would be magnified, indeed, eagerly hoping that the trappings of monarchy would now rain down upon her. She was sure her rival had thought this all up deliberately in order to show her up once and for all in front of Huldbrand and the whole world. She scolded Undine, she scolded the two old people, giving vent to her anger with bitter words: 'She has betrayed me and she has paid you to help her!'

The old fisherwoman spoke quietly to herself, 'Oh God, she has grown into an evil woman; and yet I can feel it in my heart: she is my child.' The old fisherman, for his part, held his hands together in prayer, silently pleading that this creature was not his daughter. White with horror, Undine staggered from the parents to Bertalda, from Bertalda to the parents, all at once plunged from the Heaven she had hoped for into such depths of fear and horror the like of which she had never imagined possible. She screamed over and over again in the face of her furious friend as if trying to force her to her senses after a sudden madness or a crazed nightmare:

'Do you have a soul, Bertalda? Do you truly have a soul?' Bertalda merely became even more uncontrollably angry as the rejected parents began to weep loudly. Meanwhile, the assembled company had begun to argue and had railed itself into two opposing camps. Undine felt compelled to act and demanded with both dignity and gravity the right to be heard in her husband's house, and, indeed, all fell silent around her as if a signal had been given. Then, with humility and pride, she approached the head of the table where Bertalda had been sitting, and, with all eyes fixed upon her intently, she began to speak:

'People, see how your hostility, your outrage, has torn apart my lovely celebration. In God's name, I knew nothing of your ridiculous customs and your hard nature and I doubt that I shall ever grow accustomed to them as long as I live. It is not my fault that I have done things the wrong way; believe me, the fault is all yours, whether you are willing to admit it or not. In truth, I have little to say to you, but there is one thing that must be said: I have spoken the truth. I cannot and will not give any proof other than my word, but I will swear to it. I was told by the very person who tempted Bertalda away from her parents into the water and later placed her in the path of the duke in the green meadow.'

'She is a sorceress,' cried Bertalda, 'a witch who is in league with evil spirits! She admits it herself.'

'That I do not,' said Undine, an entire Heaven of innocence and assurance in her eyes. 'Nor am I a witch; just look at me.'

'So she lies and boasts,' added Bertalda, 'and cannot prove that I am the child of these lowly people. My noble parents, I beg of you, take me away from these people and this town where they seem intent upon reviling me.'

The old, honourable duke stayed where he was, however, and his wife said, 'We must know just where we stand. I swear in God's name that I shall not put a foot out of this room until we do.'

With that, the old fisherwoman approached, bowed deeply before the duchess and said, 'You have spoken to my heart, noble, God-fearing lady. I must tell you, if this evil young girl is my daughter then she has a birthmark shaped just like a violet between her shoulder blades and another just like it on the instep of her left foot. If you would be so good as to leave the room with me.'

'I will not bare myself in front of a peasant woman,' said Bertalda, turning her back on her proudly.

'But you will in front of me,' replied the duchess gravely. 'You will follow me into that chamber, young lady, and this worthy old woman shall come too.' The three of them disappeared and everyone else remained behind in expectant silence. After a short while the women returned. Bertalda was deathly pale as the duchess spoke, 'Right is right; I therefore proclaim that our honourable hostess has spoken the truth. Bertalda is the daughter of the fisherfolk and that is as much as you need to know.' With that, the noble couple left, taking their ward with them; a signal from the duke bade the fisherman and his wife to follow. The other guests took their leave, some in silence, some muttering to themselves. Undine sank, sobbing heavily, into Huldbrand's arms.

CHAPTER 12

Departure from the Imperial City

The master of Ringstetten would, of course, have preferred it if the events of recent days had taken a different course; but, nevertheless, he could not help being pleased that his charming wife had behaved herself with such piety, good nature and warmth. 'If I have given her a soul,' he had to concede, 'then I have given her one that is far better than my own.' Now his only thoughts were of how to console the distraught young woman and to ensure that, the very next day, they might take their leave of a place which, after all that had happened, must be quite unbearable for his dear wife. It was not that her actions had been wholly unexpected, as most people had already sensed something extraordinary in her, and so the strange revelation of Bertalda's origins had not caused such a great uproar. Indeed, most people, when they heard the story, were angered by Bertalda's unseemly conduct and took Undine's part. The knight and his wife were, however, unaware of this; and anyway, the people's sympathy would have pained Undine as much as any condemnation and so the couple had little choice but to leave the walls of the old city behind them as soon as they possibly could.

As the first rays of morning sun began to break through, an elegant little coach drew up outside their lodgings to collect Undine; alongside were the knight's horses who stamped their hooves on the cobblestones as they waited for Huldbrand and his knaves. As the knight led his wife from the door, they encountered a fisher-girl standing in their path. 'We have no need of your wares,' Huldbrand said to her, 'we are about to depart.' At this, the fisher-girl began to weep bitterly and only then did the couple realize that it was Bertalda. They went straight back inside with her and heard how the duke and duchess had been so angry with her harshness and severity the day before that they had washed their hands of her completely, although not before providing her with a rich dowry. The fisherman had also been well rewarded and, by the previous evening, he and his wife had already begun their journey back to the peninsula.

'I wanted to go with them,' she continued, 'but the old fisherman who they say is my father –'

'He truly is, Bertalda,' interrupted Undine. 'Listen, the man you took to be the master of the fountain told me the whole story himself. He wanted to persuade me not to take you to Castle Ringstetten – that is when he gave the secret away.'

'Well then,' said Bertalda, 'my father – if it must be – my father said: "I will not take you with us until you have changed. Make your own way to us through the enchanted wood; that shall be the test to prove whether or not you truly care for us. But do not come to me dressed as a lady, come dressed as a fisher-girl!" And so I must do as he says; for I have been abandoned by the whole world. I shall live a lonely life with my impoverished parents and die a poor fisher-girl. Of course, I am very frightened of the wood. They say that there are terrifying ghosts in there and I am so easily scared. But what else can I do? I only came here to beg the forgiveness of the noble Lady Ringstetten for my unseemly behaviour yesterday. I realize that you did what you did with the best of intentions, dear lady, but you could not know how much your actions would hurt me, and, in my shock and surprise, I fear I may have uttered many a terrible and ill-considered word. Forgive me, please! I am already so unhappy. Think how it all was yesterday morning, as your celebrations began, and look at me now!'

The words poured forth in a stream of sorry tears. Weeping just as bitterly, Undine embraced Bertalda. She was so deeply moved that it was a while before she could bring herself to speak; but then she said, 'You must come to Ringstetten with us; everything shall be just as we planned it before; but, please, call me Undine and not madam or dear lady! Remember, we were exchanged as children; even then our destinies were entwined and now we shall entwine them so closely that no human power will be able to tear them apart. But first to Ringstetten! We shall discuss the plans for a life together as sisters once we are there.' Bertalda looked up at Huldbrand timidly. He felt sorry for the dear, distressed young girl; he reached out a hand to her and spoke to her comfortingly, placing himself and his wife at her disposal.

'We shall send a message to your parents,' he said, 'to tell them why you have not come.' He was about to add more about the worthy fisherfolk but decided against it when he saw how Bertalda cringed with pain at the very mention of them. He took her arm and lifted her into the coach, Undine after her. Then he trotted merrily alongside, urging the coachman on so that the lands surrounding the imperial city and all its sad memories were soon behind them. The ladies trundled on through the beautiful countryside in far better spirits.

Then, one beautiful evening, after a few days' travel, they arrived at Castle Ringstetten. The knight's stewards and vassals had much to report so Undine found herself alone with Bertalda. The pair strolled along the high ramparts of the castle and looked with delight at the charming countryside that lay all around in the blessed land of Swabia. They were approached by a tall man who greeted them politely and who Bertalda thought looked remarkably like the master of the fountain. The similarity became even more apparent when Undine gestured to him angrily, indeed, almost threateningly, to go away. He made off hastily, shaking his head as he had done before, this time vanishing into a nearby thicket. 'Do not be afraid, dear Bertalda,' said Undine, 'this time the hateful fountain master will do you no harm.' Then she proceeded to tell her the whole story: who she was; how Bertalda had been taken from the fisherfolk; and how she had been put in her place. At first the young woman was horrified; she thought her friend had been overcome by a sudden madness. Nevertheless, she gradually became convinced that Undine was telling the truth, partly convinced by the young bride's tale, which seemed to fit so well with past events but, above all, persuaded by that sixth sense through which the truth never fails to make itself known to us. It seemed most odd to her that she should now be living in the middle of a fairy tale to which she had previously only listened. She stared at Undine with reverence but could not overcome the sense of unease that had now come between herself and her friend. As they gathered for their evening meal, she pondered how it was that the knight could behave so lovingly and kindly towards a being who, in the light of these recent revelations, seemed to her to be more spirit than mortal.

CHAPTER 13

Life at Castle Ringstetten

The writer records this tale because it moves him and because he wants others to be moved by it too. He now asks you, dear reader, to indulge him. Forgive him if he seeks to describe what is a lengthy period of time in only a few words and only recounts in the most general of terms that which occurred. He understands very well that one could go about such a task far more skilfully, describing how, little by little, Huldbrand's affections began to be drawn away from Undine towards Bertalda. Perhaps he ought to tell how Bertalda encouraged the young man with growing affection and how they both began to fear rather than sympathize with the poor wife, whom they increasingly regarded as a mysterious creature. He might also try to explain how Undine wept and how her tears played on the knight's conscience, but failed to rekindle the old flame, and how the knight, while still treating her amicably, soon found himself driven by a cold sense of dread away from Undine and towards the human child; all of this, the writer is aware, could be described in full; indeed, perhaps it should be. Yet it pains him too much to do so, for he too has experienced such things and, in his memory, he still fears their shadow. No doubt you are acquainted with some similar emotion, dear reader, for such is the fate of all mortal beings. How lucky the soul who has endured more pain than he has inflicted, for in this respect it is surely more blessed to receive than to give. If it is so, then the mention of such things will drive naught but a sweet pain through your soul and, perhaps, allow a tender tear to trickle down your cheek in mourning for the withered bed of flowers that once delighted you so. But that is enough of such talk; we do not wish to see the heart thus wounded, as if by a thousand tiny daggers, and shall, therefore, mention but briefly the events that unfolded in the way I have already described. Poor Undine was deeply saddened, yet nor were the other two happy; Bertalda, in particular, thought she could feel the jealous pressure of the wronged wife each time things went slightly against her will. Consequently, she acquired a most commandeering manner, which was invariably supported without question by the dazzled Huldbrand and to which Undine surrendered with melancholy resignation. Castle life was further disrupted by all manner of strange ghostly apparitions, which were all at once wont to accost Huldbrand and Bertalda in the dark passageways of the castle and the like of which had never been seen in living memory. The tall white man, whom Huldbrand knew only too well as Uncle Kühleborn, Bertalda as the fountain master, often made his threatening presence felt to the pair; mostly, however, to Bertalda, so much so that she had on more than one occasion fallen in a faint on the floor and sometimes thought of leaving the castle. Yet she stayed, partly because she loved Huldbrand too much and, as there had never been an actual declaration of their mutual affection, was able to take solace in her innocence, and partly because she had no idea where else she should go. The old fisherman had replied to Huldbrand's message concerning Bertalda's whereabouts in an almost illegible scrawl of the sort common to old age and long-established custom. The message read as follows: 'I have now become a poor old widower, for my dear loyal wife has died. As my only wish now is to remain here alone in the hut, I would rather Bertalda was there than here with me. But do not let her harm my dear Undine! Otherwise, may my curse be upon her.' These final words washed over Bertalda, but, as people often tend to do in such cases, she took careful note of the part about staying away from her father.

One day, Huldbrand had just ridden out, when Undine gathered the servants together and had them bring a huge stone, which she ordered them to place carefully over the magnificent well that stood in the middle of the castle courtyard. The people protested that this would mean having to bring water up from far down in the valley. Undine smiled sadly. 'I am sorry that you will have more work, dear children,' she replied. 'If I could, I would carry the water up myself, but this well must be sealed. Believe me, there is no other solution. This is the only way to avoid an even greater ill.' The servants were pleased to be of service to their gentle mistress; no more questions were asked and they set about lifting the huge stone. They raised it up with their hands and it was hovering just above the well when Bertalda came running out and shouted at them to stop; that was the well from which she had water brought for washing. It was so good for her skin and she would never allow it to be sealed. But this time Undine remained unexpectedly firm, albeit maintaining her usual gentle manner; she said that as the master's wife it was her place to give the orders for the running of the house in the way she thought best and no one was in a position to overrule her other than her husband himself.

'Look,' cried Bertalda, anger and fear in her voice, 'the poor dear water is churning and writhing; it does not wish to be hidden from the sun and from the happy sight of peoples' faces for whom it is made to be a mirror!' And it was true, the water in the well was hissing and bubbling and behaving in the strangest manner; it was as if something were trying to force itself out, but Undine merely insisted with increased gravity that her command be carried out. Her grave tone proved quite unnecessary. The castle servants were just as happy to obey their gentle mistress as they were to defy Bertalda, and no matter how wildly she scolded and threatened, a short while afterwards the stone lay over the opening to the well. Undine leaned over it thoughtfully and began to write on the surface with her delicate fingers. She must have had something sharp and corrosive in her hand as she did so for when she turned away and the others gathered round to see, they found all manner of strange symbols on the stone that no one had seen the like of before.

Upon his return that evening, the knight was met by Bertalda, who tearfully bemoaned Undine's behaviour. He glared at his wife and the poor woman looked sadly at the floor. Then, with great composure, she began to speak: 'My lord never punishes any servants before he has heard them out, let the same be said of his behaviour towards his own wife.'

'Tell me what drove you to such an inexplicable act,' said the knight, his face darkening.

'I would like to speak with you alone!' sighed Undine.

'You can tell me just as well in Bertalda's presence,' he replied.

'If you say so,' said Undine, 'but please do not make me! Please, please do not!' She looked so humble, so lovely and obedient, that a glimmer of distant sunshine from better times shone into the knight's heart. He took her gently by the arm and led her to his chamber where she began to speak:

'You know my evil Uncle Kühleborn, dear sir, and have often crossed him in the passageways of this castle. He has, on occasions, even caused Bertalda to faint in terror. It is because he has no soul; he is a mere mirror of the elements of an outer world, which has no understanding of how to reflect the inner world. He has seen that you are dissatisfied with me, has heard me weep over it in my childish way, and noticed too that, perhaps even at the same time, Bertalda happens to be laughing. He then wrongly imagines all manner of things and meddles uninvited in our affairs. Where is the use in scolding him? What good will it do to send him away with harsh words? He does not believe a word I say. In his wretched life, he has no idea that love's pains and joys are so alike, so closely bound, that no power can separate them. A smile can break through tears just as tears are often urged forth by a smile.' Smiling tearfully, she looked up at Huldbrand, whose heart was filled once more with all the magic of his old love. Sensing this, she pressed herself close to him and, tears of joy running down her cheeks, continued to speak:

'If words will not force our trouble-maker to leave, then I must make sure he is turned away at the door and the only door through which he can reach us is that well. He has quarrelled with the other water spirits around here, in the neighbouring valleys and beyond. It is only much further up the Danube, once some of his good friends have made their way there, that his rule can take effect again. So I had the stone placed over the well and then inscribed symbols upon it that cancel all his powers so that he shall no longer cross my path, nor yours nor Bertalda's. The stone can, of course, be lifted off again with the normal effort despite the symbol; it does not hinder other people. If you wish to do as Bertalda wishes then you can, but believe me, she does not know what she is asking. That unruly Kühleborn has singled her out and if some of his prophesies were to come true, then even without you having intended any ill, oh dearest, you would not be safe either!'

Huldbrand was deeply touched by his wife's generous nature. He saw how she had taken such care to estrange her fearsome protector and yet had still felt the brunt of Bertalda's ill temper. He held her lovingly in his arms and, his voice trembling with emotion, said, 'The stone shall stay where it is and everything shall remain and should ever remain as you wish it, my dear Undine.' She caressed him humbly, glad to hear the long-sought-after words of love.

Then she said, 'My beloved friend, as you are so exceptionally good and gentle today, dare I ask something of you? You see, in many ways you resemble the summer who, even when his glory is at its greatest, wears a crown of beautiful thunderstorms, which mark him out as a rightful king and god of this earth. You too show your anger from time to time and lightning flashes from your lips and eyes and it becomes you, but from time to time you make me weep. Please, never do such a thing when we are on water or when there is water near by, for, you see, then my relatives would claim the right over me. They would take it as an insult to one of their kin and would show no mercy in tearing me from you and I would have to spend the rest of my life down there in the glass palace and would never be allowed to see you again. If they were to send me to you, then, oh God, it would be infinitely worse. No, no, sweet friend, never let it come to that, if you love poor Undine at all.'

He swore to do as she asked and the couple emerged from the chamber, endlessly happy and filled with love. Just then, Bertalda appeared with the workmen she had gathered together in the meantime. In her now customary ill-natured manner, she said, 'So, now that your secret little chat is over, perhaps the stone can be removed. Men – get to work.'

The knight was outraged at her manner and replied curtly, 'The stone stays put.' Then he reprimanded Bertalda for having ill-treated his wife. On hearing this, the workmen left, smiling to themselves with barely disguised pleasure. Bertalda became quite pale and set off in the other direction towards her chamber.

It was time for the evening meal and Bertalda was nowhere to be seen. They sent for her; her chambermaid found her quarters empty and brought only a sealed letter addressed to the knight. He opened it urgently and read:

' "It is with great shame that I have come to realize I am but a poor fisherman's child. I have allowed myself to forget this at times and must now seek repentance in my parents' lowly hut. May God grant you peace with your lovely wife!" '

Undine was deeply saddened. She begged Huldbrand fervently to hurry after her missing friend and bring her back. But she had no need to plead! His feelings for Bertalda were once more passionately aroused. He raced through the castle, demanding to know whether anyone had seen which way the beautiful runaway had flown. Unable to discover anything, he was already on his steed in the courtyard, with the intention of riding straight back the way he had come with Bertalda, when a young squire appeared and assured him that he had met the young woman on the path that led to the Black Valley. Following the youth's directions, the knight sped off at once through the castle gates. He could not hear Undine's worried cries as she called to him from the window, 'The Black Valley? Oh, not that way! Huldbrand, not that way! Or, for God's sake, at least take me with you!' When she realized that all her cries were in vain, she called hastily for her white mare to be saddled and, without taking any servants to accompany her, set off after the knight at a gallop.

CHAPTER 14

How Bertalda Rode Home with the Knight

The Black Valley lies deep in the mountains. What they call it nowadays is impossible to tell. In those days, the country folk named it after the impenetrable darkness cast by the shadows of the high pine trees. Even the stream that trickled between the rocks looked quite black and not nearly as merry as water usually does when it has the clear blue sky above it. Now, as dusk fell, it had become really very wild and dark between the hills. The knight galloped fearfully along the banks of the stream; he began to worry that his hesitation had allowed the runaway to get too far ahead or that he might miss seeing her in his haste if she were to try to hide from him. He had gone quite far into the valley and would have expected to have caught up with her by now, were he on the right track. The thought that he might not be made his heart beat even more fearfully. As the dark, stormy night drew in over the valley with growing menace, he wondered where the delicate Bertalda would shelter if he could not find her. Then he saw something white shimmering through the branches on the mountainside. He thought he recognized Bertalda's gown and made his way towards it. His horse, however, refused to go any further; it was rearing up quite violently and so, sensing he had no time to waste – the undergrowth would have hindered him too much on horseback anyway – he dismounted and tied the snorting steed to an elm tree. Having done so, he carefully worked his way through the undergrowth. The branches, wet with the cold damp of the evening dew, struck him unkindly in the face; a distant clap of thunder rumbled on the other side of the mountains; everything suddenly seemed so odd that he even began to fear the white figure that now lay quite close by on the ground. Yet he could quite clearly tell that it was a sleeping or unconscious woman in a long white gown just like the one Bertalda had worn that day. He stood next to her and rustled the branches. Then he rattled his sword – she did not move. He repeated her name, quietly at first, but then ever louder – she did not hear him. When, finally, he shouted her name at the top of his voice, a hollow echo rumbled back at him from the rocky caves of the valley, 'Bertalda!' – but the sleeping girl refused to stir. He stooped down beside her; the darkness of the valley and the failing light meant her features could not be seen. No sooner had he knelt down close to her on the ground, a terrible sense of foreboding growing in his mind, than a flash of lightning lit up the whole valley. He found himself face to face with a quite hideous countenance, which cried out to him in a hollow voice:

'Give me a kiss me then, you lovelorn shepherd.' Huldbrand leapt to his feet, screaming in horror, the hideous figure after him. 'Be gone!' she muttered, 'for the demons are awake. Be gone! Or I shall have you!' With that, she made a grab for him with her long white arms.

'Treacherous Kühleborn,' cried the knight, recovering his courage, 'what do you matter to me, you goblin? Go on, here is a fitting kiss for you!' He rushed furiously at the figure with his sword, but the apparition vanished into thin air. The gush of water that subsequently drenched him left the knight in no doubt as to the identity of the enemy he had just crossed swords with.

'He wants to frighten me away from Bertalda,' he said to himself aloud. 'He thinks I am afraid of his foolish tricks and that I will abandon that poor terrified girl to him so that he can have his revenge. But he shall not have it! Such an unworthy spirit! That powerless trickster has no idea what he is up against. He cannot conceive the courage of a human heart that desires something so much that it would gladly give its last breath to have it.' He sensed the truth of his words and felt his courage bolstered by them. It seemed too as if luck had at once joined forces with him for he had not quite reached the spot where his horse was tethered when he clearly heard Bertalda's anguished voice crying out to him from near by through the deafening roar of the storm. He hastened towards the sound and found the trembling young girl as she tried to clamber upwards in an attempt to somehow escape the terrible darkness of the valley. He stood in her path and tried to comfort her. As bold and proud as her earlier decision to leave had been, nothing could compare with the sense of relief and happiness that Bertalda now felt at the sight of her beloved friend. He had come to save her from this terrible solitude and return her to the carefree life in the old familiar castle that now seemed to reach out to her with welcoming arms. She followed almost without speaking, but was so exhausted that the knight was glad when finally he had led her to his steed. He began to untether the animal so that he might lift the errant beauty into the saddle and guide her carefully back through the unfamiliar shadows of the valley.

The horse, however, had become quite wild after witnessing Kühleborn's terrible appearance, so much so that even the knight would have had trouble in mounting this wild snorting beast; it was quite impossible to raise the trembling Bertalda into the saddle and so they decided to return home on foot. Leading the horse by the reins, the knight supported the faltering girl with his other arm. Bertalda summoned as much strength as she could in order to cross the terrible valley but exhaustion weighed her down like lead. Her every limb was trembling, partly as she recovered from the terror with which Kühleborn had driven her onwards and partly too in continuing fear of the howling thunderstorm that swept through the trees on the mountainside.

Eventually, she slipped from Huldbrand's guiding hand and sank down on the mossy ground. 'Leave me here, noble sir,' she said. 'I repent my foolish ways and must now surely perish through exhaustion and fear on this very spot.'

'I shall never leave you, dear friend!' cried Huldbrand, trying in vain to control the unruly steed, which had begun to stomp and seethe even more; in the end, the knight was just relieved that he was able to hold the beast far enough away from the kneeling woman that she should not be terrified further. He made to move away a little with the crazed horse, at which she began to call after him in utter misery, believing that he really was about to abandon her here in the terrible wilderness. He was unsure what to do for the best. He would have happily released the furious animal into the night to spend its fury, had he not feared that in this narrow pass it might thunder over the very spot where Bertalda lay with its iron-clad hooves.

In the middle of all this danger and uncertainty, Huldbrand was indescribably relieved to hear the sound of a cart slowly making its way up the stony path behind him. He called for help; a man's voice replied asking for patience but promising help. Soon after two white horses could be seen gleaming through the undergrowth; alongside them, the carter's white apron, followed by the great white tarpaulin that covered the wares he carried around with him. A loud 'Steady!' from their master brought the two white horses to an obedient halt. He approached the knight and helped him bring the foaming animal under control. 'I know what the problem is,' he said. 'When I first began travelling in this area, my two were not much better. There is an evil water nymph living here who loves to play tricks. But I learned a little saying; with your permission, I will say it in your steed's ear, then it will stand as still as my two white horses here.'

'Do what you can, but quickly!' screamed the impatient knight.

The carter pulled the head of the rearing horse down towards him and whispered a few words in its ear. All at once the steed stood quite tamely and calmly, its breathless panting and rising steam the only signs of its recent agitation. There was little time for Huldbrand to inquire how this had been achieved. The carter agreed to take Bertalda on the cart, where, so he said, she might rest on bales of the softest cotton. He would take her as far as Castle Ringstetten and the knight would accompany them on horseback. However, his steed seemed too exhausted by his earlier upset to carry his master so far and so the carter convinced him to sit in the cart with Bertalda. The horse could be tied on behind. 'It is all downhill,' he said, 'it will be easy work for my white horses.' The knight took his advice and climbed into the cart with Bertalda; the steed followed on patiently behind and the carter strode heartily and respectfully alongside. In the silence of the darkening night, as the storm rumbled off into the distance, and greatly comforted by the feeling of security and the prospect of a restful journey, Huldbrand and Bertalda were soon deep in conversation. He scolded her gently for having run off in such a contrary manner; his words moved her and she apologized so humbly that the knight could be left in no doubt that this beloved creature was still his own. He drew solace from the sense of her words far more than he regarded their meaning and it was from the sense alone that he drew his response. Suddenly the carter screeched at the top of his voice, 'Come on, horses! Walk on! Pull yourselves together! Remember what you are!' The knight leaned out of the cart and saw that the horses were striding onwards and, indeed, almost swimming, surrounded by foaming water. The cartwheels glistened and rushed like mill-wheels as the carter climbed on to the axles to escape the rising water.

'What kind of road is this?' Huldbrand shouted to his driver. 'It goes straight through the river!'

'No sir,' laughed the latter, 'it is just the opposite. The stream is flowing right across our path. Look around you, see how everything is flooded.'

Indeed, the whole valley basin swam with gushing water. It had risen all at once and they could see it was rising still further. 'This is the work of Kühleborn, the evil water spirit who wants to drown us!' cried the knight. 'Is there no saying that will ward him off, my friend?'

'Oh, I might know one,' said the carter, 'but I cannot and shall not use it until you know who I am.'

'This is no time for riddles!' cried the knight. 'The water is rising higher all the time! What does it matter to me who you are?'

'I should think it matters quite a lot to you,' said the carter, 'for I am Kühleborn.' His contorted face turned, grinning, towards them as they sat in the cart, only the cart was no longer a cart, the white horses no longer white horses; everything foamed up and ebbed away into hissing waves and even the carter reared up like a giant wave in the air, dragging the vainly struggling steed down into the flood. He then rose up once more, high above the heads of the floating couple, like a watery tower, and was about to engulf them without hope.

Just at that moment, Undine's sweet voice rang out through the roar. The moon came out from behind the clouds and, as it did so, Undine could be seen standing on the mountainside. She shouted, shaking her fist at the torrent. The terrifying towering waves ebbed away, muttering and murmuring, and the water trickled quietly away in the moonlight. They saw Undine swoop down from the high ground like a white dove. She grasped hold of the knight and Bertalda and lifted them up to a patch of lush green grass high on the mountainside where she comforted them, her words reviving their failing hearts and calming their anxious fears. She then helped Bertalda on to the white mare that had carried her there and all three returned to Castle Ringstetten.

CHAPTER 15

The Journey to Vienna

With all of this behind them, life in the castle was quiet and peaceful. The knight grew to appreciate even more the heavenly goodness that his wife had revealed so magnificently through her efforts to pursue and then rescue them from the Black Valley, the point where Kühleborn's power resumed. Undine herself felt a sense of peace and security, her soul safe in the knowledge that she was on the right path, her husband's reawakened love and respect filling her with hope and joy. Bertalda displayed gratitude and reverence, but not in such a way that she might be suspected of seeking to profit from her humility. Each time the couple tried to explain about the well or the Black Valley, she begged them fervently to stop for the very thought of the well filled her with nothing but shame, the valley with nothing but fear. So she discovered nothing more about either; and, indeed, why should she? Peace and happiness now clearly resided once more at Castle Ringstetten. They were quite sure of it and thought that life would now bring them nothing but sweet blossoms and fruit.

Winter came and went and life carried on in this delightful way. Then spring arrived to greet the happy circle with its green shoots and its clear blue sky. The new season seemed just as delighted with them as they were with it. Little wonder, then, that the sight of storks and swallows in flight awakened the wanderlust in them! One day, as they sauntered upstream towards the source of the Danube, Huldbrand began to describe how magnificent the noble river was and how it grew as it flowed through many a fortunate land. He spoke of how Vienna could be seen rising, gleaming and glorious, above its banks, and how, with every inch of its journey, the river grew in power and beauty. 'Would it not be wonderful to sail downstream all the way to Vienna!' enthused Bertalda before returning, blushing silently, to her now customary timid humility. Undine was deeply moved by this and, overcome by a keen desire to make her friend happy, she said:

'What is there to hinder us from making such a journey?' Bertalda leapt in the air for joy and, almost immediately, the two women began to imagine the delightful trip down the Danube in all its bright colours.

Huldbrand was also happy with the idea, only once voicing his concern in Undine's ear, 'Will this not hand power back to Kühleborn?'

'Just let him come,' she replied laughing, 'I will be there and he would not dare do any damage in my presence.' And so, the final obstruction was removed. They prepared for the journey and set off soon after with renewed courage and the brightest of hopes.

Yet, do not be surprised if, in the end, things turn out quite differently than planned. That treacherous power which lurks, waiting to destroy us, takes pleasure in singing its intended victims to sleep with sweet songs and golden fairy tales. In contrast, the messenger sent from Heaven to save us often knocks loudly and frighteningly at our door.

During the first few days of the journey on the Danube they were all exceptionally happy. Everything seemed better and more beautiful the further they sailed down the proud flowing river. However, no sooner had they arrived, in what seemed an otherwise charming spot whose pleasing appearance seemed to promise a great deal, than the unruly Kühleborn once more began to meddle quite openly in their affairs. At first, there were merely a few teasing tricks. Undine scolded the rising waves or the contrary wind and succeeded in taming the savage adversary for a little while. But the attacks persisted and Undine was forced to reproach them over and over again so that the enjoyment of the small party was quite disturbed. Furthermore, the crew began muttering among themselves uncertainly, watching the three gentlefolk with growing mistrust. Even their own servants began to feel that something was amiss and regarded their master with suspicion. Huldbrand kept thinking to himself, This is what happens when you do not keep to your own, when human and mermaid join together. He made excuses for himself, as people tend to do: I was not to know she was a mermaid. The misfortune is mine, that with every step I am plagued by the whims and torments of her mysterious kin, but the fault is not my own. His thoughts seemed to give him strength but his dark mood worsened and his animosity towards Undine began to grow. Soon, he found himself glaring at her sullenly; the poor woman understood the significance of this only too well. Towards evening, exhausted by these unhappy relations with her husband and the continual effort of restraining Kühleborn's antics, she sank into a deep slumber, rocked to sleep by the gentle motion of the boat.

Yet, she had barely closed her eyes when everyone on board, no matter which side they happened to be looking out from, claimed to see a quite hideous human head emerging from the waves. It did not move like the head of someone swimming but sat quite upright as if it had been driven into the surface of the water but yet was still floating along with the boat. They all wanted to show the others what frightened them and, in trying to do so, encountered the terrified faces of their companions, each pointing and staring in another direction to wherever they thought the half-laughing, half-threatening monster was. As they were still trying to tell each other about it, amid cries of, 'Look over there!', 'No, over there!', the entire hideous collection of faces suddenly became visible to everyone and the whole water around the ship swarmed with the most terrible figures. Undine was awoken by the screams of terror that ensued. As soon as she opened her eyes, the mass of miscreant faces disappeared. Huldbrand was beside himself with rage at these horrid tricks and was about to begin cursing wildly when he was interrupted by Undine's quiet voice as she humbly pleaded, 'For God's sake, husband, we are on the water, please do not become angry with me now.' The knight was silent. He sat down and fell into deep thought. Undine bent down to him and said, 'Would it not be for the best, my dear, if we were to end this tiresome journey and return to Castle Ringstetten in peace?'

Huldbrand muttered irritably, 'So, am I to be prisoner in my own castle? Only able to breathe as long as the well is closed? I wish your ludicrous kin would —' Undine covered his mouth with her soft hand. He fell silent and stayed calm, contemplating some of what Undine had said to him earlier.

Meanwhile, Bertalda's head was spinning with all manner of strange thoughts. She knew a great deal about Undine's origins and yet not everything. In particular, the awful Kühleborn had remained a terrible and still quite unfathomable mystery, so much so that she did not even know his name. As she considered all the odd things that had happened, and without really thinking, she unfastened a golden necklet that Huldbrand had bought from a pedlar to give to her on one of their last outings. Half dreaming, she let it dangle close to the surface of the water, captivated by the shimmering light reflected in the clear evening water. Suddenly a great hand shot out from the Danube, seized the necklet and carried it off under the waves. Bertalda screamed out loud and a scornful laughter could be heard echoing from the depths of the river. The knight could no longer contain his anger. Jumping to his feet, he shouted into the water, cursed all those who dared to meddle in his affairs and his life and challenged them, nix or siren, to face his drawn sword. Meanwhile, Bertalda wept over the loss of the trinket she had loved so dearly. Her tears inflamed the knight's anger. Undine held her hand in the water over the side of the boat, softly murmuring to herself, only occasionally interrupting her secret whisper to plead with her husband, 'My dearest, do not scold me here, shout at whatever you want to but not at me, not here. You know why!' And indeed his tongue, stammering with rage, held back any word that went directly against her. Then, raising the dripping wet hand she had held in the water, Undine brought forth a beautiful necklet of coral, which glistened so brightly that they were almost blinded by it. 'Take it,' she said kindly, offering it to Bertalda. 'I had this brought to replace the one taken from you. Please do not be sad any more, poor child.' Seeing this, the knight intervened. He tore the lovely piece from Undine's hand, thrust it back into the river and cried out in burning rage:

'So, you are still in league with them! Then you can keep your gifts! In the name of all evil spirits, stay with them and leave us humans in peace, you deceiver!'

Poor Undine stared at him with tears streaming down her face, her hand still outstretched. She began to weep bitterly with the innocence of a deeply aggrieved child. Then, in a feeble voice, she said, 'Oh, dear friend, I wish you well! They shall not harm you; but you must stay true if I am to keep them away from you. Oh, but I must go, even though my life is new. Alas, alas, what have you done! Alas, alas!'

With that, she slid over the edge of the boat. No one knew whether she had climbed into the water or whether she had seeped from the boat into the crystal waves; it seemed like both, or neither. Soon, however, she had trickled away into the Danube completely; all that remained was the whispered sound of sobbing from the tiny waves around the boat. They almost seemed to be saying, 'Alas, alas! Stay true! Alas!'

Huldbrand lay on the deck, burning tears running down his face. A deep swoon soon enveloped the unhappy man in its comforting veil.

CHAPTER 16

What Happened to Huldbrand Thereafter

The sorrow of man is but a fleeting pain. Whether this is to the good or otherwise, I would not like to say. By sorrow, I mean the truly deep sorrow that stems from our very souls; the sorrow that comes to truly embody the loved one who has been lost, so much so that they no longer remain lost but are rendered instead in the form of a sacred image, which we carry with us through life until the barrier that has fallen before them falls before us too. There are, of course, those in life who strive to maintain such images but even so their sorrow never quite matches the first hours of grief. Other new images force themselves among the old; we grow accustomed to earthly mortality, even in our grief, and so I must conclude: 'How unfortunate that our sorrow is but a fleeting pain!'

The master of Ringstetten discovered this too: whether or not it did him any good, we shall find out as this story unfolds. At first, he could only weep bitter tears, just as poor, dear Undine had done when he tore from her hands the gleaming trinket with which she sought to make amends. Time and time again he would stretch out his hand just as she had done and weep at her loss. He secretly hoped that he too would dissolve in tears and simply wash away; and is it not true that many of us who have suffered greatly have had similar thoughts in our distress? Bertalda joined in his mourning and for some time they lived peacefully together at Castle Ringstetten, commemorating Undine's memory and quite forgetting the feelings they once had for each other. Undine often appeared to Huldbrand in his dreams; she stroked him softly and kindly and then departed once more, weeping silently, so that when he woke, he often did not know how his cheeks had come to be wet: were the tears hers or merely his own?

As time went on the faces appeared less frequently in his dreams and Huldbrand's misery diminished. Yet he would probably have been content to live out his life in quiet remembrance of Undine, speaking of her from time to time and keeping her in his thoughts, were it not for the unexpected arrival at Castle Ringstetten of the old fisherman with the earnest demand for the return of his daughter Bertalda. He had heard of Undine's disappearance and he was no longer prepared to condone her living alone in the castle with the unmarried knight. 'Whether my daughter loves me or not,' he said, 'I do not care, but there is the question of respectability to be dealt with and that is the only consideration.'

The old fisherman's conviction and the feeling of loneliness that threatened to overcome the knight in the halls and passageways of the castle were Bertalda to leave combined to reawaken what had until then lain dormant and forgotten in the misery following Undine's loss: Huldbrand's love for the beautiful Bertalda. The fisherman protested vehemently against the planned marriage. The old man had loved Undine very much and he argued that it was far from certain that the missing girl was actually dead. Furthermore, if her corpse did indeed lie stiff and cold on the bed of the Danube or had been swept out to sea by the current, then Bertalda was partly to blame for her death and it was unseemly for her to take the place of the woman she had ousted. Yet, the fisherman was also very fond of the knight; the pleas of his daughter, who had become much softer and more submissive, coupled with her grief at the loss of Undine, brought him to the point where he felt he had to give his consent. He withdrew his objections and remained at the castle. A messenger was sent to fetch Father Heilmann, the priest who had blessed Undine and Huldbrand in earlier happy times, so that he might officiate at the knight's second betrothal.

Barely had the good man read the letter from the master of Ringstetten than he set off for the castle, his haste greater than that of the messenger sent to fetch him. When his lungs failed him or his limbs ached with fatigue as he rushed along, then he said to himself, 'There may be a terrible wrong to hinder, do not give up until you have reached your goal, oh aged, withering body!' He dragged himself up with renewed vigour and forged on without stopping to rest until, late one evening, he entered the leafy courtyard of Castle Ringstetten.

The bridal couple sat arm in arm beneath the trees. The old fisherman sat pensively at their side. No sooner had they recognized Father Heilmann than they leapt to their feet and rushed to welcome him. But without saying very much at all the priest asked to see the groom inside the castle; seeing Huldbrand hesitate in his surprise, the good clergyman said, 'Why should I wait to speak to you secretly, Ringstetten? What I have to say affects Bertalda and the fisherman just as much and, as they must hear it eventually anyway, they might as well hear it now. Are you quite sure, Knight Huldbrand, that your first wife is dead? I am not so convinced. I do not wish to comment any further on the strange tale of your relationship with her; I can be certain of nothing. But she was a God-fearing, loyal woman, that much is true. Every night for the last fortnight she has stood by my bed in my dreams, wringing her tender hands in anguish and sighing repeatedly, "Oh, stop him, dear Father! I am still alive! Please, save him! Please, save his soul!" I did not understand what the dream meant; then your messenger arrived and I came here as quickly as I could. I have come not to join, but to tear asunder that which does not belong together. Leave her, Huldbrand! Leave him, Bertalda! He still belongs to another. Can you not see how grief for his lost wife still haunts his pale cheeks? This is not how a groom should look, and the spirit tells me, "Even if you do not leave him, you will never be happy with him." '

All three were sure in their hearts that Father Heilmann spoke the truth but they did not want to believe it. Even the old fisherman was by now so beguiled that he felt they must carry through the plans laid in recent days. In desperation, they argued with the clergyman until he eventually took his leave of the castle, sadly shaking his head, refusing to accept shelter for the night or any of the comforts they offered him. Huldbrand managed to convince himself that the clergyman's head must be full of silly notions. The next morning he sent to the local abbey for a priest, who promptly promised to bless the couple within the next few days.

CHAPTER 17

The Knight's Dream

In the hours between night and daybreak, the knight lay half waking, half sleeping on his bed. Each time he was about to fall asleep, an unknown fear seemed to hold him back, chasing him away from the phantoms that were lurking in his slumbers. Yet if he tried to wake up properly, then things swirled around him, flapping like swans' wings, with the comforting sound of lapping waves, and lulled him back into a half-sleep. When he finally seemed to have fallen into a deep sleep, it was the fluttering swans that seized him and carried him on real wings far away over land and sea, singing all the while in the sweetest voice: 'Swan cry! Swan song!' and he kept saying to himself, 'That must mean death?' But, most likely, it had another meaning. All at once it was as if he were floating above the Mediterranean Sea and as he looked down into the waters, they were transformed into a thousand crystals so that he could see right down to the bottom. He was delighted, for he could see Undine sitting beneath the glass vaults. Of course, she was weeping and looked far sadder than in those happy days when they had lived together at Castle Ringstetten, especially at the beginning and later even, just before they had begun the wretched trip on the Danube. This made the knight think carefully about all that had happened, but Undine did not seem to realize he was there. In the meantime, Kühleborn had appeared and was about to reprimand her for her weeping. She gathered herself and looked at him with such a noble, commanding air that he was almost afraid. 'Even if I am living here under the water,' she said, 'I am still in possession of my soul. I am, therefore, quite entitled to cry, even if you have no idea what tears are. They are sacred, as is everything that has a soul.'

He shook his head in disbelief and, after pausing to think, said, 'Very well, but remember, niece, you are still subject to our elemental laws and must still punish him by death if he ever remarries or is disloyal to you.'

'He is still a widower to this day,' said Undine, 'and loves me from the bottom of his grieving heart.'

'But at the same time he is a groom,' laughed Kühleborn mockingly. 'In a few days the church ceremony will be over and then you will have to ascend to ensure the bigamist's death.'

'But I cannot,' smiled Undine in reply. 'I sealed the well, it remains closed to me and my kin.'

'Yes, but what if he leaves his castle,' said Kühleborn, 'or if he ever had the well reopened! For I am sure he thinks precious little of such things.'

'For that very reason,' said Undine, smiling despite her tears, 'for that very reason he is now floating in spirit above the Mediterranean, dreaming this conversation as a warning. I purposely had it happen this way.' Kühleborn glared angrily up at the knight, stamped his feet and shot like an arrow straight under the waves. It was as if he had swollen up with evil to the size of a whale. The swans began to sing again, to flap and to fly; the knight felt as if he was floating over alps and rivers, floating finally into Castle Ringstetten where he woke in his bed.

He did indeed wake up in his bed. His knave had just arrived to tell him that Father Heilmann was still near by; he had met him the night before in the forest, sheltering in a hut, which he had constructed from tree branches and lined with moss and twigs. When asked why he was still there if he did not intend to officiate at the marriage ceremony, he had replied, 'There are other ceremonies than those at the bridal altar and if I am not come for the wedding, then perhaps for something else. We must wait and see. Anyway, weddings and funerals have much in common and those who do not wilfully seek to ignore this, can see it very well.'

The knight was given over to all manner of strange thoughts as he considered these words and the events in his dream, but it is always very difficult to alter something once a person has it fixed in their mind, and so everything remained as before.

CHAPTER 18

Knight Huldbrand's Wedding

If I were to tell you what happened at Castle Ringstetten on the night of the wedding feast, then you would do well to imagine a thousand shining trinkets draped in a black shroud, under whose sombre veil the manifold riches had the appearance of having been gathered not in celebration but in mockery at the worthlessness of the earthly pleasures we all desire. Yet it was not that some ghostly monster had upset the mood of celebration, for we know that the castle was a haven from the tricks of the threatening water spirits. Instead, it seemed to the knight and the fisherman, and indeed to all the guests, that the most important person was missing, and that person was dear, kind Undine. Every time a door opened, all eyes turned involuntarily towards it, and when it then proved to be simply the butler bringing some new dish or the waiter with yet more fine wine, then everyone gazed sadly ahead, the occasional sparks of joviality and joy once more extinguished by the dew of wistful remembrance. The bride was the most carefree of all and therefore also the merriest; but even she began to find it odd that she should be sitting at the head of the table, adorned with a lush garland and clad in a gold-embroidered gown, while Undine lay, stiff and cold, on the bed of the Danube, or was being driven by the current far out to sea. Ever since her father had spoken these words, they had rung over and over in her ears and, today more than any other, would not be silenced.

The wedding party dispersed just before nightfall, the celebration not brought to an end by the eager hopes of an impatient groom, as is often the case on such occasions, but the guests instead forced apart in sadness by a morbid melancholy and a sense of impending doom. Bertalda went with her maids, the knight with his knaves, to prepare for the wedding night but there was none of the customary joviality among the escort of young men and women at this sad feast.

Bertalda wanted to cheer herself up: she ordered the magnificent set of jewellery that Huldbrand had given her to be laid out along with her rich gowns and veils so that she might choose the most becoming and cheerful attire for the following day. This gave her maids the welcome opportunity to express their joy and delight and, in so doing, they did not fail to praise the newly-wed's great beauty. These observations went on at some length until, eventually, Bertalda let out a deep sigh as she gazed in the mirror, 'Oh, but just look at this blemish appearing here on the side of my neck!' They looked and, indeed, it was as their beautiful mistress said, but they declared it to be an endearing mark, a little patch that heightened the paleness of her tender skin. 'I would be rid of it easily,' she sighed, 'but the castle well, from which I once drew the precious cleansing water, has been sealed. If I only had a bottle of it today!'

'Is that all?' laughed her sprightly maid as she slipped out of the chamber.

'Surely she will not be so reckless as to have the stone removed from the well this very night?' asked Bertalda in utter amazement. Yet, the sound of men crossing the courtyard could soon be heard and they watched from the window as the eager maid led them towards the well, levers and other equipment hoisted on their shoulders. 'Well, it is not as if I did not wish it,' smiled Bertalda, 'as long as it does not take too long.' Happy in the knowledge that a mere hint on her part had this time sufficed to achieve what had previously been so painfully denied to her, she looked on as the work proceeded in the moonlit courtyard below.

The men lifted the stone with a great deal of effort; now and again one or two of them must have let out a sigh, remembering that they were now destroying the work of their dear departed mistress. Yet, the task proved much easier than expected. It was as if some power within the well was helping to hoist the stone aloft. The workmen turned to one another in amazement. 'It is as if the water inside had turned into a fountain,' they said. Indeed, the stone began to rise higher and higher in the air and, almost without any assistance from the labourers, rolled slowly away, landing on the cobbles with a dull thud. Then, almost at once, what looked like a white column of water rose majestically from the opening of the well. At first they thought it really was a fountain until they saw that the rising figure was that of a pale, white-veiled woman. She wept bitterly, wringing her hands in anguish as she raised them above her head. She walked solemnly towards the castle. The servants ran from the well in all directions; the bride stood pale, transfixed in terror at her window with her servants. As the figure passed below, it looked up at her, whimpering, and Bertalda thought she could make out Undine's pale face under the veil. The miserable figure walked on, slowly and hesitantly, as if on the sad final walk to execution. Bertalda screamed for someone to summon Huldbrand but none of the servants dared move from the spot. Even the bride was silent once more as if shaken by the sound of her own voice.

As they remained at the window, terrified, like motionless statues, the strange wanderer entered the castle. She made her way up the old familiar stairway and walked through the old familiar halls, weeping silently as she went. Oh, how different things had once been for her here!

The knight had excused his servants. Half undressed, he stood before a huge mirror, his mind deeply troubled; the candle burned feebly beside him. He heard a familiar soft knocking at the door, just as Undine had done when she wanted to come to him. 'It is just my mind playing tricks!' he said to himself. 'I must go to my wedding bed.'

'That you must, but it shall be a cold one!' The tearful voice came from beyond the chamber. Still looking in the mirror, Huldbrand saw the door open very slowly and the white wanderer entered, closing the door behind her. 'They have opened the well,' she said quietly, 'and now I am here and you must die.' He knew in his failing heart that what she said was true. He covered his eyes with his hands and said:

'Do not drive me mad with fear in my final hour. If your veil hides a vile and hideous face, then please do not lift it; kill me without me seeing you.'

'Oh,' replied the wanderer, 'do you not want to see me one last time? I am as beautiful as I was when you courted me on the peninsula.'

'Oh, if only it were so!' sighed Huldbrand; 'would that I could die with a kiss from your lips.'

'With pleasure, my dear,' she said. She pushed back her veil to reveal her lovely face smiling with heavenly beauty. Trembling with love and at the closeness of death, the knight bowed towards her, she kissed him with a heavenly kiss and did not let him go. She held him ever closer to her breast and wept as if she wanted to weep her soul away. The tears fell into the knight's eyes and flowed like a sweet pain through his veins until the breath finally went from his body and he slid softly from her tender arms on to the soft pillows of his bed.

She met some servants standing in the antechamber. 'I have wept him to death!' she said as she walked slowly out through the crowd of terrified onlookers towards the well.

CHAPTER 19

How Knight Huldbrand was Buried

Father Heilmann arrived at the castle as soon as news of the death of the master of Ringstetten became known, and indeed almost at the very same moment that the monk who had married the unhappy couple fled, overcome with fear and horror, from the castle gates. 'So it should be,' said Heilmann when he heard of this. 'Now my duties are about to begin and I require no assistance.' He then began to comfort the widowed bride, although it was of little use to her worldly, thoughtless nature. The old fisherman, on the other hand, although deeply saddened, could far better comprehend the fate that had befallen daughter and son-in-law, and while Bertalda could not stop declaiming Undine as a murderer and a sorceress, the old man said calmly:

'It could not have been otherwise. I see no more than God's judgement and no one can have been more upset by Huldbrand's death than she who was forced to carry it out, poor, abandoned Undine!' He helped to organize the funeral in a manner befitting the rank of the deceased. Huldbrand was to be buried in a nearby village in the graveyard where all his ancestors lay and which his family had generously honoured with many gifts and freedoms. His shield and helmet lay on the coffin ready to be lowered into the crypt with him, for the master of Ringstetten was the last of his line. The mourners began their painful procession, their lament rising up into the calm blue sky as Heilmann led the way with a tall cross; the inconsolable Bertalda, supported by her aged father, followed on behind. As they walked after the widow, the black-clad mourners suddenly became aware of a snow-white figure wearing a heavy veil, her hands raised aloft in wretched anguish. Those who found themselves walking beside her felt a strange horror come over them, they moved back or to the side, their movement frightening others who then found themselves next to the white stranger so that, soon after, all manner of disorder began to break out in the funeral procession. One or two soldiers were brave enough to confront the figure and to try to separate her from the procession, but she slipped from their hands and was soon to be seen among the mourners once more, walking on slowly and solemnly. Eventually, as the others continued to avoid her, she found herself close to Bertalda. Undine kept pace slowly and carefully behind Bertalda so that the widow would not notice her, and she continued to walk on humbly and orderly behind her.

This went on until they had reached the churchyard and the procession closed in a circle round the open grave. Then Bertalda saw the uninvited escort and, roused half in anger, half in fear, asked her to leave the knight's resting place. The veiled figure shook her head softly and raised her hands towards Bertalda as if pleading humbly. This moved the latter greatly and made her think tearfully of the kindness with which Undine had wanted to give her the coral necklet on the Danube. Just then Father Heilmann held up his hand and demanded silence so that prayers might be said in silent remembrance of the deceased as the coffin was being covered. Bertalda fell silent and knelt down and they all knelt, the grave-diggers too, once they had finished their task. As they rose again, the white stranger had vanished; on the spot where she had knelt, a bright silver stream flowed from the grass, and kept trickling on until it had almost encircled the knight's grave; then it ran further and poured into a still pool by the churchyard. Many years later, so the story goes, the inhabitants of the village still pointed to the stream, firm in their belief that it was poor, rejected Undine whose kindly arms still embraced her lover.

The Tale of Honest Casper and Fair Annie

CLEMENS BRENTANO

It was early summer. A few days before the nightingales had once more begun to fill the air with their delightful song. That night they had been silenced by the cool evening breeze, which brought far-off storms towards us. The night-watchman had just called eleven when I saw a motley company of young men gathered by the entrance of a large building. They were on their way home after an evening of merriment and had assembled round a figure who was sitting on the steps. So animated was their concern that I feared some misfortune and approached.

An old peasant woman sat calmly on the stair. Despite the lively concern of the young men, she remained aloof from their inquisitive questions and well-meaning suggestions. Indeed, there was something quite odd, if not positively grand, in the way that the old woman remained intent upon her own purpose. It was as if she were alone in her own little chamber as she made herself comfortable for a night under the stars with all these people round her. She wrapped her apron round her like a little cloak, pulled her black wax-linen hat further over her eyes, arranged her bundle of belongings under her head and answered none of the many questions.

'What is the matter with this old woman?' I asked one of those present. Answers came from all sides: she has walked six miles from the country; she cannot go any further; she does not know her way round the town; she has friends at the other end of the town and cannot find her way there.

'I wanted to take her,' said one, 'but it is a long way and I do not have my house key with me. Anyway, she would not recognize the house where she wants to go.'

'But the woman cannot stay lying here all night,' said a newcomer to the scene.

'She flatly refuses,' answered the first. 'I told her some time ago that I would take her home, but she is talking nonsense, she must be drunk.'

'I think she must be a little mad. But surely she cannot stay lying here,' repeated the other. 'It's going to be a long, cold night.'

While all this was being said, the old woman had completed her preparations as if she were both deaf and blind, and as the latter once more said: 'She cannot stay lying here,' she responded in a strange voice, both deep and serious in tone:

'Why should I not stay here? Is this not the ducal house? I am eighty-eight years old and the duke will surely not drive me from his door. Three sons have died in his service and my only grandchild has gone too; – God will surely forgive him and I do not want to die until he has been given an honest grave.'

'Eighty-eight years and walked for six miles!' exclaimed those who stood around. 'She is tired and simple. At that age people become weak.'

'Mother, you might catch cold and become very ill here, and you will weary too,' said one of the young men as he bent down closer to her.

The old woman spoke again in her deep voice, half pleading, half commanding:

'Oh, leave me in peace and don't be so silly; I have no need to catch cold; I have no cause to be weary; time is running out, I am eighty-eight, it will soon be morning and then I will go to my friends. If a person is God-fearing and believes in destiny and does not forget to pray, then he can surely survive these few hours.'

The crowd had gradually drifted away and the last few who remained soon hurried away too as they spied the night-watchman on his rounds, for they wanted him to open their doors. I alone remained. The street was much quieter. I wandered up and down thoughtfully under the trees in the empty square before me; the manner of the old woman, her calm, serious tone, her certain knowledge of the life that she had seen unfold season by season through the course of her eighty-eight years and which to her appeared to be little more than a waiting-room in a house of prayer; all of this had affected me deeply. Of how little import are the pains, the desires of my heart, for the stars will still follow their path undisturbed; why do I seek solace and from whom do I seek it and, indeed, for whom? Whatever I seek and love and achieve on this earth – will it ever lead me to a state as peaceful as that good, God-fearing soul, to be able to spend the night in the doorway of a house until morning comes and, even then, will I find that friend as she will? Nay, for I would not even reach the town, I would already have collapsed, travel weary, in the sand at the gates, and might even have fallen foul of ruffians and thieves. These were my thoughts as I made my way through the avenue of lime trees back towards the old woman. I heard her praying, half out loud to herself, with her head bowed. I was strangely moved as I approached her: 'While you are with God, mother,' I said, 'say a little prayer for me!' and with these words I threw a thaler into her apron.

The old woman spoke very softly: 'A thousand thanks, dear Lord, for listening to my prayer.'

I thought she was speaking to me: 'Mother, did you ask me for something? I didn't hear.'

The old lady rose to her feet in surprise: 'Dear sir, go home, say your prayers well and go to bed. What are you doing wandering the streets? That is no way for a young man to live, for the enemy is afoot and looking for prey. Many have met their end during such night walks. Whom do you seek, sir? The Lord is in a man's heart, as long as he lives decently and not on the street. If the gentleman is looking for the enemy, though, then he is lost already. Go home now and pray and you shall be rid of him. Good-night.'

After she had spoken these words she turned her self round very slowly to face the other way and put the thaler in her bag. Everything that the old woman did made a peculiarly serious impression upon me and I said to her: 'Dear mother, you are most likely quite right, but it is you yourself who keep me here; I heard you praying and wanted to ask you to pray for me too.'

'That is already done,' she said, 'for when I saw you walking through the lime trees I asked God to grant you good thoughts. Now you have them, so go off nicely to bed.'

Instead I sat down next to her on the step, took hold of her thin hand and said: 'Let me sit here with you through the night. Tell me where you have come from and what it is you are seeking here in the town. There is no one to help you here. At your age one is nearer to God than to other people; the world has changed since you were young.'

'I hadn't noticed,' replied the old woman. 'I have found it all to be much the same throughout my life; you are still too young, still amazed by everything; I have seen it all so often that now I am only able to see it all with such pleasure still because the Lord brings out the good in it. But one should not refuse goodwill, even if it is not really required, for then that same good friend might stay away when he is truly needed; so stay here and see if you can help me. I will tell you what it is that has brought me the long way to town. I never thought I would come here again. It is seventy years since I worked as a maid in the house, the doorstep of which I now sit upon. Since then I have not been back. How time passes! It is like the blinking of an eye. How many times I sat here in the evenings seventy years ago and waited for my sweetheart who was in the guard. We became engaged here too. When he – but, ssh, here comes the watch.'

Then she began to sing at the door in a quiet voice, just as maids and servants do on moonlit, nights, and I listened with an intense pleasure as she sang the following song:

> 'When dawn breaks on the final day,
> The stars will fall from Heaven's way.
> The dead, the dead must rise again,
> To face the final judgement's pain.
> With gentle steps you must approach
> Th' assembly of angelic host;
> The Lord came from a distant land,
> Bearing a rainbow in his hand.
> Then came the false Jews manifold
> Who our dear Lord once prisoner held.

The high tree-tops so brightly lit,
The hard stones echoed underfoot.
Whoever can recite this prayer,
Pray for the day just one time more
The soul will stand God's scrutiny,
When all go into eternity.
Amen.'

As the watch approached, the old woman became tearful. 'Alas,' she said, 'today is the sixteenth of May; it is all just the same, just as it was then, only they have different caps and no pony-tails. But what difference does it make!'

The officer of the watch stopped by us and was about to ask what we were doing here so late when I recognized him to be an acquaintance of mine, the ensign, Count Grossinger. I quickly related the events to him and, somewhat startled, he said: 'Here's a thaler for the old woman and a rose. These old peasants like flowers.' He gave me the bloom that he held in his hand. 'Ask the old woman to let you write down the song and bring it to me tomorrow. I have been after the words for a long time but have never quite been able to get a hold of them.'

Across the square, the sentry of the nearby watch, to which I had accompanied the count, cried out, 'Who goes there!' As we parted, he told me that he was on duty at the castle and that I was to visit him there. I went back to the old woman and gave her the rose and the thaler.

She took the rose with moving intensity and fastened it to her hat as she spoke, her voice far softer, almost crying:

'Roses the flowers upon my hat,
Oh, to be as rich as that,
Roses and my sweetheart.'

I said to her: 'Well, little mother, you have cheered up,' to which she replied:

'Cheery, cheery,
Ever brighter,
Ever rounder
Once above,
Now coming down,
It's no wonder.'

'Oh sir, dear sir, it wasn't a good thing I stayed here. It's all the same, believe me; it's seventy years to the day since I sat here in front of this door; I was a bright young thing and loved to sing all the songs. That night I sang the "Song of the Last Judgement", like I did just now, as the watch went by and, as they did so, a young grenadier threw a red rose in my lap – I still have the petals in my Bible – that was the first meeting with my good husband. The next morning I wore the rose to church and he found me and soon all was well. That's why I was so pleased to be given a rose again today. It's a sign that I am to join him and I am very much looking forward to that. I have lost four sons and a daughter; the day before yesterday my grandson went too – God help him and have mercy on him! – And tomorrow another good soul will leave me. But what do I mean, tomorrow, is it not already past midnight?'

'It is just past twelve,' I replied, mystified by her words.

'May God give her solace and peace in the four short hours she still has left,' said the old woman, falling silent as she folded her hands in prayer. Her words and her manner shocked me so much that I could not speak. Yet, as she remained quite silent with the officer's thaler still in her apron, I said to her:

'Mother, put the thaler in a safe place; you might lose it.'

'I don't want to put it away, I want to give it to my friend in her last hour of need!' she replied. 'I shall take the first thaler home with me tomorrow, for it belongs to my grandson and he should benefit from it. Ah yes, he has always been a lovely boy, sound in body and in soul. Oh God, his soul! – I prayed the whole way, it can't be, surely the Lord will not allow him to perish. Of all the youngsters, he was always the cleanest and the keenest at school, but when it came to honour he surpassed them all. His lieutenant always said, if there is any honour in the body of my squadron, then it is quartered with Finkel. He was with the Ulans. When he came back from France the first time, he told all manner of marvellous tales, but the talk was always of honour. His father and his stepbrother were in the home guard and often quarrelled with him over honour, for what he possessed too much of, they had too little. God forgive me my terrible sin, I do not wish to speak ill of them, we all have our cross to bear: but my late daughter, Casper's mother, worked herself to death for that layabout of a husband. She couldn't afford to pay off his debts. The Ulan spoke of the French and when his father and his stepbrother tried to criticize them, the Ulan said: "Father, you do not understand, they are most honourable!" That made his stepbrother spiteful and he said: "How is it you can preach to your father so much about honour? Was he not a sergeant in the N— regiment? He must know more about it than you do, you are only a common soldier." "Yes, indeed," said Finkel senior, who was by now quite argumentative too, "that I was, and I doled out twenty-five lashes to a few big-mouthed youngsters; if I had had Frenchmen in the company, then they would have felt them even better with all their honour." These words hurt the Ulan: "Let me tell you the story of a French sergeant. Under the previous king, corporal punishment was set to be introduced into the French army. The war minister's order was given in Strasbourg at a grand parade and the troops listened grimly to the announcement as they stood in line. At the end of the parade a common soldier behaved himself badly and his sergeant was ordered to give him twelve lashes. The order was strict and he had to do it. But when he had finished, he took the weapon of the man he had hit, stood it on the ground before him and pressed with his foot so that the bullet went through his head and he fell dead on the ground. This was reported to the king and the command for corporal punishment was revoked. You see, Father, that was an honourable man!" "He was a fool," said his brother. "To hell with you and your honour!" growled the father. With that, my grandson took his sword, left the house and came to me in my little hut and told me everything and wept bitter tears. I couldn't help him; I couldn't completely dismiss the tale he told me but, still, at the end I said to him: "Render honour to God alone!" I gave him my blessing, for his leave was at an end the following day and he wanted to make the mile-long trip to the place where a god-daughter of mine, whom he held in high esteem, was in service on the estate. He wanted to visit her. They should soon be together, if God hears my prayers. He has already gone. My god-daughter should be with him today and I have already gathered the dowry; there is to be no one else at the wedding but me.' The old woman fell silent once more and seemed to be praying. I was quite preoccupied with the thought of honour, and whether a Christian should find the sergeant's death beautiful. I hoped someone might be able to make sense of it all for me one day.

As the watchman called one o'clock, the old woman said: 'Now I have two hours; oh, you're still here, why don't you go off to bed? You won't be able to work tomorrow and you'll get into trouble with your master. What is your trade, young man?'

I was unsure how to explain to her that I was a poet. I could not very well say I was an educated man without lying. It is strange that a German always feels a little embarrassed to say that he is a poet. One says it least willingly to people from the lower classes for these are liable to associate this with the scribes and pharisees in the Bible. The name 'poet' is not so commonplace as the term *homme de lettres* is in France, where there are even writers' guilds and more traditional regulation, whereby one can even ask: 'Où avez-vous fait votre Philosophie?' – 'Where did you study Philosophy?' How much better the Frenchman is at passing himself off as a worthy man. Still, this non-German custom is not the only one that makes the word 'poet' so difficult to utter when one is asked for one's business at the door, but instead a certain inner shame holds us back, a feeling that is experienced by everyone who has to do with free and spiritual wares, with the direct gifts of Heaven. Scholars and artisans have no need to feel so ashamed as writers do for they have usually paid for their education, are usually employed in offices of the state or seek to fashion great stone slabs or work below ground to contain great torrents of water. But a so-called poet is in the worst position, because he has usually escaped the schoolyard for the Parnassus, and a professional poet is even more suspect for he does not see it as just a mere pastime.

One can quite easily say to him: every man has an element of poetry in his body, just as he has a brain, a heart, a stomach, a spleen, a liver and the like, and whoever overfeeds, ill-feeds or gorges one of these organs and does this, forsaking the others, by making it his line of business, should be ashamed of himself in the presence of his fellow men. One who lives from poetry has lost his sense of balance, and an overfed goose liver, no matter how good it tastes, requires an unhealthy goose. All people who do not earn their living with sweat on their brow must to some extent be ashamed, and that is felt by one who has not yet found himself in trouble, when forced to admit he is a poet. Many thoughts ran through my head as I considered what I should say to the old woman. She was surprised at my hesitation and looked at me:

'What is your trade, I ask, why won't you reveal it? Is it not an honest trade? If not, then you can still learn one. There is still time. Don't tell me you are a hangman or a spy here to seek me out. Be who you want for all I care! If you were sitting here like this in daylight, I would think you were a lout, one of those wastrels who leans against houses to avoid falling over for sheer laziness.'

Then it suddenly occurred to me how I could bridge the gap of comprehension between us: 'Dear mother,' I said, 'I am a writer.'

'Well,' she said, 'why did you not say so straight away? So, you are a man of the pen. For that you need a fine head, quick fingers and a good heart, otherwise you might get a rap on the knuckles. A writer, eh? Then you would be able to write me a petition for the duke, which would be certain of being heard and not lie unnoticed with the many others.'

'A petition, dear mother,' I said, 'can easily be written and I will make every effort to draft it with the utmost urgency.'

'That is very good of you,' she replied. 'May God reward you for it and let you grow older than me and, when you are old, may he give you such a sense of peace and a beautiful night with roses and coins such as this and also a friend who will write you a petition when you need it most, just as he has given me. But now go home, dear friend. Buy a sheet of paper and write the petition; I shall wait here for you another hour, then I shall go to my godchild. You can come with me.

She'll be pleased with the petition too. She truly has a good heart but the Lord's will often appears strange to us.'

With these words the old woman was silent. She bowed her head and seemed to be praying. The thaler still lay in her lap. She wept. 'Dear mother, what is the matter, what ails you so that you weep?' I asked.

'Why should I not weep! I weep for the thaler, I weep for the petition, I weep for everything. But it doesn't help. It's far, far better on this earth than we humans deserve and even bitter tears are still too sweet. Just look at that golden camel over there above the apothecary's door! See how God created everything to be so wonderful. Yet man does not appreciate it and such a camel is as unlikely to fit through the eye of a needle as a rich man is to enter Heaven. But what are you doing still sitting there! Go and buy the paper and bring the petition to me.'

'Dear mother,' I said, 'how can I write the petition when you have not told me what to write in it?'

'Must I tell you that?' she replied. 'Then yours is clearly no art to speak of, and I no longer wonder that you were ashamed to say you were a writer if it is necessary to tell you everything. Well, I shall do my very best. Write in the petition that two lovers should rest next to each other and that the body of one should not be given over to the anatomists so that they both have all their limbs together when the call goes out: "The dead, the dead must rise again,/ To face the final judgement's pain."' Then she began to weep again bitterly.

I sensed she must be overwhelmed by a deep sorrow but only occasionally did she feel herself so painfully moved by the burden of her years. She wept without sobbing, her words remained both calm and cold. I asked her once more to recount the whole story behind her trip to the town:

'My grandson, the Ulan, whom I told you about, was very much in love with my godchild, as I told you before. She was known as Fair Annie because of her quite perfect countenance. His talk was always of honour and he always told her that she should cherish her honour and also his own. And because of all this talk of honour, the girl took on quite a different air in both appearance and attire. She became more refined and affected than all the other girls. She seemed more sensitive to everything and if a young lad should hold her a little roughly when dancing, or swing her a little higher than the bridge of the double bass, then she would come to me and cry quite bitterly, saying always that it went against her honour. Oh, Annie was always a strange girl. Sometimes, just when you least expected it, she would grab at her apron with both hands and rip it from her as if it were on fire, and then she would begin to weep in the most awful way. But there was a reason for that. It drew her with its teeth. The enemy does not rest. If only the child had not always been so interested in honour, and had instead kept faith with the Lord. Would that she had never let him leave her in her greatest need and had borne both shame and rejection for his sake, instead of seeking to preserve her honour. God would surely have forgiven her, and still would. Oh, they must surely rest together, let it be God's will.

'The Ulan was billeted in France again. He had not written for a long time and we almost believed him to be dead and often wept over him. He was, however, in hospital with a serious wound and, as he rejoined his comrades and was promoted to sergeant, he remembered how his stepbrother had snapped at him two years before, saying that he was only a common soldier and his father a sergeant; and then he remembered the story about the French sergeant and how much he had spoken to Annie about honour before he had left. He could not rest with these thoughts in mind and became quite homesick. When his cavalry captain inquired what was wrong, he said: "Oh, sir, I feel as if something were pulling me home with its teeth." And so they let him ride home with his horse, for all his officers trusted him. He was given three months' leave and was to return for the *remonte*. He hurried as fast as he could without hurting his horse, whom he cared for more than ever now that it had been entrusted to him. One day the urge to be home was quite terrible. It was the day before the anniversary of his mother's death and it was as if she were running in front of his horse and calling: "Honour me, Casper!" Ah, I sat alone on the grave for a long time that day and thought, If only Casper were here with me. I had woven a garland of forget-me-nots and hung it on the sunken cross and measured myself out a space and thought, This is where I want to lie, and that is where Casper should lie if God grants him a grave in his homeland. Then we shall be together when the call goes out: "The dead, the dead must rise again, / To face the final judgement's pain." But Casper did not come, nor did I know he was so close by and that he could have come. He was driven along in great haste for he had often thought of this day when he was in France and had brought with him a garland of lovely golden flowers to adorn his mother's grave and a garland too for Annie, which she was to keep until her birthday.'

With that, the old woman fell silent and shook her head. As I repeated the last words: ' "Which she was to keep until her birthday," ' she spoke again:

'Perhaps if I were to beg or plead. Oh, if only I could waken the duke!'

'Why?' I asked, 'what are your requests, mother?'

She spoke earnestly: 'What would be the point of life, if it never came to an end? What would be the point of life, were it not eternal!' With that she continued her tale:

'Casper would have arrived in our village well before midday, but that morning his host drew his attention to the condition of his horse. It was quite dejected. The innkeeper said: "My friend, that is not the sign of an honourable rider." These words affected Casper deeply. He placed the empty saddle on the animal's back and fastened it only lightly, doing everything to spare the wound, and recommenced his journey on foot, leading the horse by a rope. And so it was already late in the evening when he came to a mill a mile from our village. Recognizing the miller as an old friend of his father, he called in and was received as a most welcome guest from abroad. Casper led his horse into the stall, laid the saddle and the knapsack in a corner and went to the miller in his room. First he asked after his family and listened as the miller told him that I, the old grandmother, was still alive, that his father and stepbrother were both in good health and that they were doing well. Only yesterday they had been at the mill with grain. His father had entered the livestock business and was making a good living at it. He now cherished his honour and no longer went about so unkempt. This pleased Casper greatly. Then he asked after Fair Annie. The miller said to him that he did not know her but if it was the girl who used to be in service at the Rosenhof, then she had, so they said, gone to work in the town, because she preferred to go and learn something there and it was more honourable to do so. That was what he had heard a year ago from the stable-boy at the Rosenhof. This pleased Casper too, even if, at the same time, it hurt him that he would not see her straight away, but he hoped to find her soon in the city, all prim and proper, so that it would be a real honour for a sergeant to go out walking with her on a Sunday. Then he told the miller a few tales of France as they ate and drank with one another. He helped him to spread the corn and then the miller showed him to a bed in the upper room and then went himself to sleep on some sacks down below. The working of the mill and the desire to be at home meant that, despite being very tired, Casper was unable to sleep properly. He was very restless and thought of his late mother and of Fair Annie and of the honour he would feel at being able to greet his family as a sergeant. He dozed only lightly and was often startled by fearful dreams. Several times he thought he saw his late mother coming towards him, wringing her hands and pleading with him for help, for it seemed to him as if he had died and was being buried, on his way to his own grave on foot, a dead man, with Fair Annie by his side. He was weeping loudly because his comrades were not with him, and as he came to the churchyard, he saw that his grave was next to that of his mother and Annie's grave was there too. He gave Annie the garland that he had brought for her and he hung the one for his mother on her grave and then he looked around and could see only me. Annie had been pulled by the apron into the grave. Then he climbed into the grave too and said: "Is there no one here who will do me the final honour of shooting me, that I might fall into my grave like a brave soldier?" Then he drew his pistol and fired. The shot awoke him with a start for it seemed as if the windows were rattling. He looked around the room, then he heard another shot and a scuffle in the mill and shouting above the sound of the machinery. He leapt from his bed and seized hold of his sword. Just then the door flew open and, in the light of the full moon, he saw two men with soot-darkened faces approaching him with clubs. He made to defend himself and struck one above the arm, at which they both fled but not before they had bolted the door, which opened outwards, from the outside. Casper tried in vain to go after them. He finally succeeded in kicking in one of the door panels and hastened through the hole and down the stairs, where he heard the miller's cries of pain. He found him bound and gagged, lying between the sacks of corn. Casper untied him and then rushed straight to the stable to look for his horse and knapsack but they were both gone. He rushed back into the mill in great distress and bemoaned his misfortune to the miller. All his worldly possessions had been stolen and, even worse, the entrusted horse. It was all too much. However, the miller stood before him with a bag full of money which he had taken from the cupboard in the upper room and said to the Ulan: "Dear Casper, have no fear, I must thank you for saving my property. The robbers were after this bag, which was upstairs in your room, and I have you to thank for saving it. Nothing was stolen. Those who took your horse and knapsack from the stable must have been acting as lookouts for the thieves. They signalled with their shots that there was danger. I expect they saw from your tack that there was a cavalryman in the house. You must suffer no inconvenience for my sake, I will make every effort and spare no means to find your steed again and if I cannot then I will buy you another, no matter how much it costs." Casper replied: "I will accept nothing as a gift for it goes against my honour, but if you could, in my hour of need, lend me seventy thaler, then you shall have a written promise that the sum will be repaid in two years." They agreed on this and the Ulan departed. He hastened onwards to his village to inform the sheriff of the events. The miller stayed at home to wait for his wife and son, who were at a wedding in a nearby village. Then he intended to follow the Ulan and lodge a report with the sheriff too.

'You can imagine, dear writer, poor Casper's dismay as he made his way to our village, on foot and impoverished, having once wished to ride in with such pride; the fifty-one thaler which he had saved, his sergeant's commission, his leave papers and the garlands for his mother's grave and for Annie had all been stolen. He felt quite confused when he arrived home at one o'clock in the morning and immediately knocked at the door of the sheriff, whose house is the first on the outskirts of the village. He was shown in and made his complaint, listing everything that had been stolen from him. The sheriff instructed him to go straight to his father, who was the only farmer in the village who owned horses. He was to cover the area with his father and his brother to see whether they could perhaps find any trace of the robbers. In the meantime, the sheriff would send others out on foot and take down the rest of the details when the miller arrived. Casper then left the sheriff and made for his father's house. However, as he was passing my little hut on the way there, he heard me singing a hymn through the window. I could not sleep for thinking about his late mother. He knocked and said: "Praise the Lord, dear grandmother, it is me, Casper." Oh, how those words touched my very soul! I stumbled to the window, opened it and kissed and embraced him in floods of tears. He quickly told me of his misfortune and explained the instructions for his father from the sheriff. He must go there right away and track down the thieves, for his honour depended on his retrieving the horse.

'I am not sure why, but the word "honour" chilled my very bones for I knew that harsh judgements awaited him. "Do your duty and render honour to God alone," I said. Leaving me, he hastened towards Finkel's farm, which lay at the other end of the village. I sank to the ground on my knees as he left and prayed to God that He might protect him. Oh, I prayed as never before in my fear, and kept saying over and over again: "Lord, may your will be done on earth as it is in Heaven."

'Casper was filled with a terrible sense of fear as he ran to his father. As he climbed over the garden fence, he could hear the pump working. All at once he heard a whinnying from the stable, which went through his very soul. As he stood there in the moonlight, he saw two men washing themselves. He felt as if his heart was about to break. One of them spoke: "This damn stuff is hard to shift!" Then the other said: "Come into the stable first. We need to chop off the horse's tail and cut its mane. Have you buried the knapsack deep enough in the muck?" "Yes," replied the other. With that they went to the stable and Casper, quite mad with misery, jumped out and closed the stable door behind them. He cried out: "In the name of the duke! Give yourselves up. I will shoot anyone who struggles!" He had captured his father and his stepbrother. They were the thieves who had stolen his horse. "My honour, my honour is lost!" he cried. "I am the son of a dishonourable thief." As the pair in the stable heard his voice, they became angry and cried: "Casper, dear Casper, for God's sake, you will ruin us! Casper, you shall have everything back, for your mother's sake. Today is the anniversary of her death. Have pity on your father and your brother." But Casper was quite distraught and simply kept shouting: "My honour, my duty!" And as they then tried to force the door open, and pushed a beam into the clay wall in order to escape, he fired his pistol in the air and shouted: "Help, help, thieves, help!" The farmers, who had by now been woken by the sheriff, were already near-by, discussing the different ways in which they might pursue the men who had robbed the mill. They came rushing into the building at the sound of the gunshot and Casper's cries. Old Finkel was still pleading with his son to open the door. The son, for his part, said: "I am a soldier and must serve justice." At that the sheriff arrived with the farmers. Casper said: "May the Lord have pity on us, sir, my own father and brother are themselves the thieves. Oh, how I wish I had never been born! I captured them here in the stable, my knapsack is buried in the muck." On hearing these words, the farmers sprang into the stable and tied up old Finkel and his son and took them back to their house. Casper dug out the knapsack and took out the two garlands. Instead of going to the house, he went to the churchyard and sat by his mother's grave.

'By now day had dawned. I had been in the meadow and had woven two garlands of forget-me-nots for myself and for Casper. I thought: "He shall join me in adorning his mother's grave when he returns." Then I heard all manner of uproar in the village and, because I do not care for such turmoil, I made my way round the village to the churchyard. There was a shot; I saw the vapour rise in the air. I hurried to the churchyard. Oh dear Saviour! Have mercy on him. Casper lay dead on his mother's grave. He had shot himself in the heart. He had fastened Fair Annie's garland to the button over his heart and fired the shot right through it. The garland for his mother was already fastened to the cross. As I beheld this sight, it felt as if the earth below me was opening up. I threw myself on him and cried over and over again: "Casper, oh you poor, unhappy man, what have you done? Oh, how did you learn of your misery? Oh, why did I let you go, before telling you everything. Oh Lord, what will your poor father and your brother say when they find you like this?" Of course, I did not know that they were the cause of his actions. I thought there was another reason. Then things became worse. The sheriff and the farmers brought old Finkel and his son tied with a rope. I could barely speak, I was so upset. The sheriff asked me whether I had seen my grandson. I pointed to where he lay. He approached Casper and, thinking he was weeping on the grave, the sheriff shook him. Then he saw the blood. "Jesus, Mary!" he cried out. "Casper has taken his own life!" The two prisoners looked at each other in terror. They took Casper's body and carried it alongside them to the sheriff's house. Cries of mourning filled the whole village. The farmers' wives helped me along behind. Oh, that was surely the most awful journey of my life!'

Then the old woman fell silent again and I said to her: 'Dear mother, you have suffered terribly, but God must truly love you, for those he tries sorely are his most beloved children. Now tell me, what moved you to travel this long distance and what do you wish to make the subject of your petition?'

'Oh, you can most probably imagine,' she continued quite calmly. 'I wish for an honourable burial for Casper and Fair Annie. Look, I brought this garland to mark her birthday. It bears Casper's blood.'

She pulled a small garland of gold foil from her bundle and showed it to me. In the dawn light I could see that it was blackened by gunpowder and splattered with blood. I was deeply moved by the misfortune of the good old woman, and the dignity with which she bore it all filled me with admiration. 'Dear mother,' I said, 'How are you going to break this news to poor Annie without her falling down dead in fright? What makes this day so special that you chose it to bring Annie this sad memento?'

'Dear sir,' she said, 'just come with me, you can accompany me on my way to see her. I can't move quickly, so we will reach her just in time. I will explain everything to you on the way.'

With that she stood up and said her morning prayer quite calmly. Then she straightened her clothes and hung her bundle over my arm.

It was two o'clock in the morning and day was breaking as we wandered through the silent streets.

'You see, sir,' she continued, 'when Finkel and his son were locked up, I went to see the sheriff in the courtroom. Casper's body was brought in and laid out on a table, covered with his Ulan coat. Then I had to tell the sheriff everything that I knew about him and what he had said to me that morning through the window. He wrote it all down on the paper that lay before him. Then he looked through the notebook that they had found with Casper. There were some calculations in it, a few tales of honour, including the one about the French sergeant, and at the back there was something written in pencil.'

She gave me the notebook and let me read Casper's last unhappy words: 'Even I cannot survive this shame. My father and my brother are thieves, they even robbed me. It broke my heart but I had to capture them and hand them over to the authorities, for I am a loyal soldier and my honour allows me no mercy. I have handed my father and brother over to be punished for the sake of honour. Oh! Someone pray for me, please. Pray that they grant me an honourable grave here next to my mother. I want my grandmother to send the garland that felt the fatal shot to Fair Annie and give her my regards. Oh! I pity her from the bottom of my heart but she must not marry the son of a thief, for she has always cherished her honour so. Dear, beautiful Annie, do not be afraid when you hear about me. Accept it, and if you wish to grant me only the smallest favour, then do not speak ill of me. I cannot help my shame! I had gone to such lengths to uphold my honour my whole life through. I was already a sergeant and had earned the best name in the squadron. I would surely have been made an officer one day. Even then, Annie, I would never have left you. I would have found none better. But the son of a thief who had to capture his own father and let him be hanged for honour's sake – who could survive such a scandal. Annie, dear Annie, please take the garland; I have always been true to you. May God have mercy on me! I now give you back your freedom, but do me the honour and never marry a lesser man than me; and, if you can, then plead for me that I might be given an honourable grave here next to my mother, and if you should die here in our own village then ask to be buried here with us; our kindly grandmother will come to us too one day and then we shall all be together. I have fifty thaler in my knapsack, which are to be saved with interest for your first child. My silver watch is for the priest; my uniform and weapon belong to the duke; this notebook is yours. Farewell my beloved, pray for me and may you all live in peace! May God forgive me – oh, how great is my despair!'

I could not read these, the last words of such an obviously noble yet unfortunate man, without shedding bitter tears. 'Casper must truly have been a good man, dear mother,' I said.

On hearing my words, she stood still, held my hand tightly and said in a voice trembling with emotion: 'Yes, he was the best man in the world. But those last words, the part about desperation, he should never have written them. They will rob him of his honourable grave. They mean he will go to the anatomical institute. Oh, dear writer, if you could only help with this.'

'Why?' I asked. 'How can it be that these last words could lead to such a thing?'

'It's true,' she replied, 'the sheriff told me so himself. An order has gone out to all the courts that only those who commit suicide through melancholy should have an honourable burial. Those who kill themselves out of desperation are to be sent instead to the anatomical institute, and the sheriff told me that he must send Casper there because he admitted himself to being desperate.'

'What a strange law,' I said. 'One could almost set up a trial after every suicide: death caused by melancholy or desperation. It would last so long that the judges and barristers would themselves descend into melancholy and desperation and end up in the anatomical institute too. But take heart, dear mother. Our duke is such a good man. When he hears the whole story, he will surely grant Casper a resting place next to his mother.'

'May God grant his will!' said the old woman. 'Once the sheriff had written everything down, he gave me the notebook and the garland for Fair Annie and I walked all the way here yesterday so that I might give her some comfort on her day of honour. Casper died at the right time. If he had known all this, he would have gone mad with worry.'

'What has happened to Fair Annie?' I asked the old woman. 'One minute you speak of her having only a few hours left, the next you speak of her day of honour and that she will find comfort in the sad news you bring. Tell me everything. Does she wish to marry another? Is she dead or ill? I must know everything so that I can put it all in the petition.'

The old woman replied: 'Oh, dear writer, it is thus. May God's will be granted! You see, when Casper came, I was not truly happy. When he took his life, I was not truly sad. I would never have been able to survive it, if God had not softened the blow with far greater suffering. It is as I say. It was as if there were a stone weighing down upon my heart, like an ice-breaker, and all the pain, which crashed against me like pack-ice and which would have doubtless destroyed my heart, broke into pieces on this stone and drifted coldly on by. I want to tell you something deeply upsetting:

'When my god-daughter, Fair Annie, lost her mother – a cousin of mine who lived seven miles away – I was with the dying woman. She was the widow of a poor farmer and in her youth she had loved a hunter but had not married him because of his unruly ways. The hunter eventually sunk to such depths that he found himself in prison for life for murder. My cousin found this out as she lay ill in bed and it upset her so much that she became worse every day and was about to die when she handed care of Fair Annie over to me and bade me farewell. In her last moments she said to me: "Dear Anne Margreth, if you should pass through the town where the poor lad is locked up, please ask the guard to tell him this. I beseech him on my deathbed to return to God. I have prayed for him with all my heart in my final hour and I send him my warmest regards." Soon after these words were spoken, my good cousin died and, once she was buried, I took Fair Annie, who was then three years old, in my arms and back to my house.

'On the outskirts of the town that I had to pass through, I came across the executioner's house and, as the master there was well known as an animal doctor, I was to take back some preparations for our mayor. I entered the room and told the master what I wanted and he replied that I should follow him up to the attic, where he had laid out the herbs, to help him choose. I left Annie in the room and followed him. When we returned we found Annie standing before a small cupboard, which was fixed to the wall: "Grandmother, there is a mouse in there, listen to it rattling about. There is a mouse in there!"

'On hearing the child's words, the master's face became very serious. He tore open the cupboard door and exclaimed: "God have mercy on us all!" For his executioner's sword, which hung alone in the cupboard on a nail, was swinging back and forth. He removed the sword and I felt a shiver run through me. "Dear madam," he said, "if you love Fair Annie, then you will allow me to make a light scratch round her neck. The sword swung back and forward before her. It demands her blood and if I do not mark her throat with it then the child shall have a life of misery before her." With that he took hold of the child, who began to scream in terror. I screamed too and pulled the child back. Just then the mayor came in. He was returning from the hunt and wanted to bring the executioner a sick dog to be healed. He asked what was the cause of all the screaming. Annie cried: "He wants to kill me!" I was utterly terrified. When the executioner told the mayor what had happened, the latter reprimanded him sharply and condemned his superstition. The executioner remained quite calm and said: "My forebears believed it and so do I." Then the mayor said: "Master Franz, if you believed that your sword had moved because I came to tell you that tomorrow at six in the morning you were to behead the hunter Jürge, then I would forgive you, but for you to wish to act upon this poor dear child is both unreasonable and mad. It could drive a person to desperation to discover in later life that something of this sort happened to them as a child. No one should be led into temptation."

'"But nor should an executioner's sword," said Master Franz to himself as he hung the sword back in the cupboard.

'Then the mayor kissed Annie and gave her some bread from his hunting bag. He asked me who I was, where I came from and where I was going. Once I told him of my cousin's death and of the message for the hunter Jürge, he said to me: "You can tell him yourself. I will take you to see him. He has a hard heart but perhaps the concern of a goodly person in his final hours will move him." Then he helped

Annie and me into his carriage, which was waiting at the door, and drove us into the town.

'He told me to go to his cook. In the kitchen we were given a good meal and towards evening he took me to see the poor sinner. When I told the hunter of my cousin's final words, he began to weep bitterly and cried: "Oh God, if only she had become my wife, it would never have come to this!" Then he requested that the priest be brought to him once more as he wished to pray with him. The mayor promised this and, praising him for his change of heart, asked him whether he had a final wish, which could be granted before his death. The hunter Jürge said: "Please ask this kindly old mother to be present at my execution tomorrow with the daughter of her blessed cousin. It will strengthen my heart in my final hour." The mayor asked me and, although it filled me with horror, I could not deny the poor, miserable man. I had to give him my hand and promise formally. He sank weeping on to the straw. Then the mayor took me to his friend the priest and I was asked to recount everything again before he went to the prison.

'I spent the night with the child in the mayor's house and the next morning began the difficult journey to attend the execution of the hunter Jürge. I stood next to the mayor in the circle and watched as he broke the rod and pronounced sentence. The hunter Jürge spoke movingly and everyone cried. He looked at me and little Annie, who stood before me, obviously filled with emotion, and then he kissed Master Franz. The priest prayed with him and then his eyes were bound as he knelt down. Then the executioner dealt the death blow. "Jesus, Mary and Joseph!" I cried out loud, for Jürge's head flew towards Annie and sank its teeth into the child's dress. She screamed in terror. I tore the apron from my body and threw it over the hideous head.

'Master Franz rushed across, snatched it from me and said: "Mother, mother, what did I tell you yesterday morning. I know my sword, it lives!" I fell to the ground in shock. Annie screamed again in terror. The mayor was quite overcome and had us taken to his house. There his wife gave me some clothes for myself and the child. Later in the afternoon the mayor gave us some money as well, as did many other people from the town who wanted to see Annie. In the end I had received twenty thaler and a great many clothes for the child. That evening the priest came and spoke with me at length. He said I should be sure to bring Annie up strictly in fear of God and ignore all the worrying signs that were simply Satan's tricks, which one must treat with contempt. Then he gave me a lovely Bible for Annie, which she still has, and the next day the mayor had us driven the last three miles home. Oh, dear Lord, and despite all of this it has still come to pass!' Then the old woman was silent.

A terrible fear gripped me. The old woman's tales had disturbed me greatly. 'For God's sake, mother!' I cried aloud. 'What has happened to poor Annie? Can nothing be done to help her?'

'It gripped her and dragged her by the teeth. She was made to do it,' said the old woman. 'She will be executed today; but she did it out of desperation. Honour was her master. Her shame was born of the desire for honour. She was led astray by a wealthy man who left her. She smothered her own child in the selfsame apron that I threw over the hunter Jürge's head that day and which she had secretly taken from me. Oh, it dragged her by the teeth and made her do it, she did it out of desperation. The seducer had promised to marry her and told her that Casper had fallen in France. She became desperate and carried out the evil deed before handing herself over to the courts. She will be executed at four o'clock. She wrote to me. I want to see her once more. I will do so now and give her the garland along with the message from poor Casper and the rose I was given last night. It will be of comfort to her. Oh, dear writer, if only you can make the case in the petition, that she and poor Casper be allowed to be buried together in our churchyard.'

'Everything, I will try everything!' I cried. 'I will go to the castle right now. My friend, the one who gave you the rose, is on watch there. He shall wake the duke for me and I will kneel before his bed and plead for a pardon for Annie.'

'A pardon?' said the old woman coldly. 'It dragged her by the teeth. Do you hear, dear friend, justice is better than a pardon; what use are all the pardons on earth; we must all face judgement one day:

'The dead, the dead must rise again,
And face the final judgement's pain.

'You see, she does not wish to be pardoned. It was offered to her
if she would name the father of the child, but Annie answered: "I
have murdered his child. I want to die, not to make him unhappy. I
must suffer my punishment so that I can be with my child, but it
would destroy him if I were to name him." And so she was condemned
to the sword. Go now to the duke and plead for an honourable grave
for Casper and Annie. Go straight away, look, there goes the priest
on his way to the prison. I want to talk with him, so that he will take
me with him to see Fair Annie. If you hurry, then perhaps you will
be able to bring us some comfort at the execution – an honourable
grave for Casper and Annie.'

As we spoke, we met up with the priest. The old woman explained
her relationship to the prisoner and he took her with him to the prison.
I made off in haste towards the castle. I ran as I had never done before.
It gave me comfort and hope to hear a beautiful voice accompanied by
a lute coming from the window of the garden house as I stumbled
passed the home of Count Grossinger:

'Mercy spoke of love
As honour still held watch,
And full of love wished mercy
An honourable good night.

'Mercy takes the veil,
The roses come from love,
Honour greets the suitor,
For the sake of mercy's love.'

There were more good omens to come. A hundred yards further
on I came upon a white veil lying on the road. I seized it. It was
adorned with perfumed roses. I held it in my hand and ran on further,
thinking: Oh Lord, mercy is come. As I turned the corner, I caught
sight of a man who hid himself in his cloak as I rushed past, and quite

clearly turned his back towards me in order not to be seen. This was quite unnecessary for I could see and hear nothing but my thoughts of mercy. I stumbled through the portcullis into the courtyard of the castle. Thank goodness, the ensign, Count Grossinger, who was pacing up and down under the chestnut tree in front of the guardhouse, was on his way towards me.

'Dear Count,' I said frantically, 'you must take me to the duke immediately, straight away, or it will be too late, all will be lost!'

He seemed embarrassed by this request: 'What are you thinking of? At this irregular hour? It is not possible. Come to inspection tomorrow and I will introduce you.'

The earth burned beneath my feet. 'Now!' I cried aloud. 'Or never! A human life is at stake.'

'Not now,' replied the count curtly. 'It is a question of my honour. I have orders not to deliver any messages tonight.'

The word 'honour' filled me with despair. I thought of Casper's honour, of Annie's honour, and said: 'Damn your honour. It is precisely because of such honour that I must see the duke, to procure assistance for a poor soul in her final hour. You must announce me now or I shall call out loud for the duke myself.'

'If you so much as move,' said Grossinger angrily, 'I will have you thrown in the guardhouse. You are quite mad! Have you no notion of propriety?'

'Oh, I know all about propriety, terrible propriety! I must see the duke, every second is precious! I repeat, if you do not announce me immediately, then I shall go to him myself.'

With these words I made for the stairway that led up to the duke's apartments, at which point I noticed the very man I had just seen wrapped in his cloak rushing up the selfsame staircase. Grossinger pulled me round roughly so that I would not see him. 'What are you doing, you fool?' he whispered to me. 'Be quiet, calm down, or you will get me into trouble.'

'Why did you not stop the man who went up just now?' I asked. 'His business can be no more pressing than mine. Oh, it is so urgent, I must go, I must! It concerns the fate of a poor, unhappy, misled creature.'

'You saw the man go up there,' Grossinger replied. 'If you say one word about it, then you will meet with my sword. You cannot go up for the simple reason that he has. The duke has business with him.'

Just then a light appeared in the duke's window. 'Lord, there is light, he is awake!' I said. 'I must speak to him, for Heaven's sake, let me go or I shall cry for help.'

Grossinger took hold of my arm: 'You are drunk, come into the guardhouse. I am your friend, get some sleep and tell me about the song that the old woman was singing at the gate tonight as I was doing my rounds. It is of great interest to me.'

'It is precisely because of the old woman and her loved ones that I must speak to the duke!' I cried.

'Because of the old woman?' asked Grossinger. 'It is because of her that you are talking to me! Noble men have no time for such things. To the guardhouse now.'

He tried to drag me away. Just then the castle clock struck half-past three. The toll of the bell cut through my soul like a cry for help and I shouted at the top of my voice up to the duke's window: 'Help, for God's sake, help a miserable, misled creature!' Grossinger was beside himself. He tried to cover my mouth but I struggled with him. He struck me on the back of the neck and cursed. For a moment it was as if I could hear nothing. He called for the guard. The corporal came quickly with a number of soldiers to apprehend me, but at that very moment the duke's window flew open and a voice called down: 'Ensign Grossinger, what on earth is all this row? Bring that person up here right now!'

I did not wait for the ensign. I leapt up the stairs, and fell at the feet of the duke, who, somewhat taken aback, bade me unwillingly to stand. He had on boots and spurs but also a night-gown, which he clasped together carefully over his chest.

As quickly as I could I blurted out everything the old woman had told me, about the Ulan's suicide and the tale of Fair Annie. I begged him to at least postpone the execution for a few hours and to grant an honourable grave for the two unhappy souls, if such a mercy were possible. 'Oh mercy, mercy!' I cried, as I took the white veil of roses from under my cloak. 'I took this veil, which I found on the way here, to be a sign of mercy.'

The duke seemed quite overcome as he reached out for the veil. He was deeply moved. He held the veil in his hands as I spoke these words: 'Your Highness, this poor girl is the victim of a false sense of honour. A rich man led her astray and promised to marry her. She is so good that she would rather die than name him –'

The duke interrupted with tears in his eyes and said: 'Silence, for Heaven's sake!' Then he turned to the ensign who stood by the door and said with great urgency: 'Go, take this man and ride with speed. Ride the horse to death if you have to! Go straight to the courthouse. Tie this veil to your weapon, wave and cry out Mercy! Mercy! I will follow you.'

Grossinger took the veil. He was much changed. In his fear and haste he had the appearance of a ghost. We ran to the stable, mounted and galloped off. He rode like a madman out of the gate. As he tied the veil to his weapon he cried: 'Lord Jesus, my sister!' I could not fathom what he meant by it. He stood in the stirrups and waved, crying, 'Mercy, mercy!' We saw a crowd gathered on the hill by the courthouse. My horse shied at the fluttering cloth. I am but a poor horseman and could not keep up with Grossinger. He rode off at full pelt while I made every effort I could to follow. But, oh how sad is fate! The artillery were exercising near by and their cannon fire made it impossible for our cries to be heard in the distance. Grossinger stormed through the crowd as the people hurried out of his path. I looked towards the circle and saw the glint of steel in the early morning sun. Oh Lord, the glint of the executioner's blade! I rode on, I heard cries of pain from the crowd. 'Let me pass, let me pass!' cried Grossinger and rode with the flowing veil into the circle like a madman, but the executioner already held aloft the bloody head of Fair Annie before him. She smiled a melancholy smile. With that the ensign cried out: 'God have mercy on me!' He fell to the ground on the corpse. 'Kill me, kill me! I led her astray, I am her murderer!'

A vengeful anger took hold of the crowd. The women and young girls pushed to the front, tore him from the corpse and began kicking him. He did not try to defend himself. The guards could not bring the furious crowd under control. Then the cry went up: 'The duke, the duke!' He arrived in an open carriage, a fresh-faced young man wrapped in a cloak sat next to him. The people pushed Grossinger forward. 'Lord Jesus, my brother!' cried the young officer in a most effeminate voice.

The duke turned to him in consternation: 'Silence!' He leapt from the carriage. The young man tried to follow but the duke pushed him back roughly. As he did so, the secret was revealed: the young man was Grossinger's sister disguised in an officer's cloak. The duke ordered that the bloody, senseless Grossinger be placed in the carriage. His sister no longer sought to disguise herself. Her womanly attire was there for all to see. The duke was embarrassed but he gathered himself and gave the command to turn the carriage immediately and take the countess and her brother home. This event had calmed the anger of the crowd to some degree. The duke turned to the officer on duty and said quite audibly: 'The Countess Grossinger saw her brother ride by their house on his way to bring the pardon and wanted to witness this happy event; as I rode by on the same errand, she stood at her window and requested that I bring her along in my carriage. I could not refuse the request from such a well-meaning child. She took her brother's cloak and hat in order not to draw attention to herself, an action which, surprised by these unhappy events, had quite the opposite effect in making it all seem like a scandalous adventure. But Lieutenant, why did you not protect the unfortunate Count Grossinger from the rabble? It is a horrendous case: it was not his fault that he arrived too late. I want to see the count's assailants arrested and punished.'

The duke's speech provoked a general outcry: 'He is a bounder and a seducer, the murderer of Fair Annie, he admitted it himself, the miserable, lowly wastrel!'

On hearing this from all sides and having it confirmed by the priest, the officer and the court officials, the duke was so deeply shocked that he said nothing except: 'How awful; a tragedy, the miserable man!'

Then, pale and white, the duke entered the circle. He wanted to see the corpse of Fair Annie. She lay on the green grass in a black dress with white ribbons. The old grandmother, who had paid no attention to the goings on around her, had placed Annie's head back on her severed neck and covered the fatal cut with her apron. She folded the dead girl's hands over the Bible that the priest had given her as a little girl. Then she tied the golden garland round her head and on her breast she laid the rose that Grossinger had given the old woman the night before without realizing who she was.

Looking on, the duke said: 'Beautiful, unhappy Annie! Shameful seducer, you arrived too late! Poor old mother, you were the only one to keep faith with her, right to the end.' Noticing me near by as he spoke, he turned to me and said: 'You mentioned Corporal Casper's last will, do you have it with you?'

I turned to the old woman and said: 'Poor mother, give me Casper's notebook. His Highness wishes to read his last will.'

The old woman was not paying attention. She spoke gruffly to me: 'So you are back then? You might as well have stayed at home. Do you have the petition? It's too late now, I couldn't comfort the poor child with the knowledge that she would lie with Casper in an honourable grave. Oh, I pretended all right, but she wouldn't believe me.'

The duke interrupted her and said: 'You did not lie, good mother. This man did his utmost. The stumbling horse alone is to blame. But she shall have an honest grave beside her mother and with Casper, who was an honourable young man. A sermon will be delivered for both of them. The honour will be God's alone. Casper will be buried as an ensign, his squadron will fire a threefold salute over his grave and the weapon of the seducer Grossinger shall be laid on his coffin.' Having spoken these words, the duke took Grossinger's weapon, which still lay on the ground with the veil. He untied the veil, covered Annie with it and said: 'This unhappy veil, which would dearly have loved to bring her mercy, shall restore her honour once more. She died honourably and with a pardon. The veil shall be buried with her.' He gave the weapon to the officer of the guards with the words: 'You will receive my orders concerning the burial of the Ulan and this poor girl later today at inspection.'

Then he read aloud Casper's last words with great emotion. The old grandmother embraced his feet with tears of joy, as if she were the happiest woman alive. He said to her: 'Rest easily now. You will receive a pension until your death and I shall erect a memorial stone to your grandson and Annie.' Then he ordered the priest to return to his home with the dead girl in a coffin and then to take the old woman home to organize the burial. Meanwhile, his adjutant had arrived with the horses. The duke turned to me and said: 'Give my adjutant your name, I shall call for you; you have acted with such laudable humanity.' The adjutant wrote down my name and complimented me sincerely. Then the duke rode on into the town with the blessings of the crowd. The body of Fair Annie was taken to the priest's house with the kindly old grandmother. The following night the clergyman travelled home with her. The officer arrived there the following evening with Grossinger's weapon and a squadron of Ulans. Honest Casper was buried with Grossinger's weapon on his coffin and with an ensign's commission. He lay next to Fair Annie at his mother's side. I too had made my way there and accompanied the old mother, who was like a child in her joy but said very little. As the Ulans fired the third salute over Casper's grave, she collapsed dead in my arms and also found her grave next to her loved ones. God grant them all a joyous resurrection!

> With gentle steps you must approach
> Th' assembly of the angelic host;
> Whence cometh the Lord our God,
> The fairest rainbow in his hand.
> Their souls will stand God's scrutiny,
> When we all go into eternity.
> Amen

On my return to the town I heard that Count Grossinger had died. He had taken poison. In my room I found a letter from him which read as follows:

I have a great deal to thank you for, you brought my shame, which had long plagued my heart, to the light of day. That song the old woman sang was well known to me, Annie sang it to me often; she was an indescribably noble creature. I was but a miserable criminal. She had a written promise of marriage from me and she burned it. She was in service with an old aunt of mine and was often melancholic. I gained control of her soul by means of certain

medicinal means which have a magical effect. May God have mercy on me! You also saved the honour of my sister; the duke loves her, I was his favourite. The story has shocked him – God help me, I have taken poison.
Joseph (Count) Grossinger.

Fair Annie's apron, which covered the head of the hunter Jürge after his execution, has been preserved in the duke's private collection. They say that the duke is going to elevate Grossinger's sister to the nobility with the title 'Voile de grace' (Veil of Grace) and marry her. At the next review of the D— area, a monument on the grave of the two unfortunate victims of honour will be erected in the village churchyard and formally dedicated. The duke himself is to attend with the duchess. He is decidedly pleased with it; they say the idea came from the duchess and the duke together. It represents false and true honour, both bowed to the earth before a cross. Justice stands to one side with a raised sword, Mercy to the other, casting a veil over it. They say that the head of Justice bears a resemblance to the duke; mercy, for her part, has the look of the duchess.

READ MORE IN PENGUIN

In every corner of the world, on every subject under the sun, Penguin represents quality and variety – the very best in publishing today.

For complete information about books available from Penguin – including Puffins, Penguin Classics and Arkana – and how to order them, write to us at the appropriate address below. Please note that for copyright reasons the selection of books varies from country to country.

In the United Kingdom: Please write to *Dept. EP, Penguin Books Ltd, Bath Road, Harmondsworth, West Drayton, Middlesex UB7 ODA*

In the United States: Please write to *Consumer Sales, Penguin Putnam Inc., P.O. Box 12289 Dept. B, Newark, New Jersey 07101-5289.* VISA and MasterCard holders call 1-800-788-6262 to order Penguin titles

In Canada: Please write to *Penguin Books Canada Ltd, 10 Alcorn Avenue, Suite 300, Toronto, Ontario M4V 3B2*

In Australia: Please write to *Penguin Books Australia Ltd, P.O. Box 257, Ringwood, Victoria 3134*

In New Zealand: Please write to *Penguin Books (NZ) Ltd, Private Bag 102902, North Shore Mail Centre, Auckland 10*

In India: Please write to *Penguin Books India Pvt Ltd, 11 Community Centre, Panchsheel Park, New Delhi 110017*

In the Netherlands: Please write to *Penguin Books Netherlands bv, Postbus 3507, NL-1001 AH Amsterdam*

In Germany: Please write to *Penguin Books Deutschland GmbH, Metzlerstrasse 26, 60594 Frankfurt am Main*

In Spain: Please write to *Penguin Books S. A., Bravo Murillo 19, 1° B, 28015 Madrid*

In Italy: Please write to *Penguin Italia s.r.l., Via Benedetto Croce 2, 20094 Corsico, Milano*

In France: Please write to *Penguin France, Le Carré Wilson, 62 rue Benjamin Baillaud, 31500 Toulouse*

In Japan: Please write to *Penguin Books Japan Ltd, Kaneko Building, 2-3-25 Koraku, Bunkyo-Ku, Tokyo 112*

In South Africa: Please write to *Penguin Books South Africa (Pty) Ltd, Private Bag X14, Parkview, 2122 Johannesburg*

READ MORE IN PENGUIN

A CHOICE OF CLASSICS

Leopoldo Alas	**La Regenta**
Leon B. Alberti	**On Painting**
Ludovico Ariosto	**Orlando Furioso** (in two volumes)
Giovanni Boccaccio	**The Decameron**
Baldassar Castiglione	**The Book of the Courtier**
Benvenuto Cellini	**Autobiography**
Miguel de Cervantes	**Don Quixote**
	Exemplary Stories
Dante	**The Divine Comedy** (in three volumes)
	La Vita Nuova
Machado de Assis	**Dom Casmurro**
Bernal Díaz	**The Conquest of New Spain**
Niccolò Machiavelli	**The Discourses**
	The Prince
Alessandro Manzoni	**The Betrothed**
Emilia Pardo Bazán	**The House of Ulloa**
Benito Pérez Galdós	**Fortunata and Jacinta**
Eça de Quierós	**The Maias**
Sor Juana Inés de la Cruz	**Poems, Protest and a Dream**
Giorgio Vasari	**Lives of the Artists** (in two volumes)

and

Five Italian Renaissance Comedies
 (Machiavelli/**The Mandragola**; Ariosto/**Lena**; Aretino/**The Stablemaster**; Gl'Intronati/**The Deceived**; Guarini/**The Faithful Shepherd**)
The Poem of the Cid
Two Spanish Picaresque Novels
 (Anon/**Lazarillo de Tormes**; de Quevedo/**The Swindler**)

READ MORE IN PENGUIN

A CHOICE OF CLASSICS

READ MORE IN PENGUIN

A CHOICE OF CLASSICS

Jacob Burckhardt	**The Civilization of the Renaissance in Italy**
Carl von Clausewitz	**On War**
Meister Eckhart	**Selected Writings**
Friedrich Engels	**The Origin of the Family**
	The Condition of the Working Class in England
Goethe	**Elective Affinities**
	Faust Parts One and Two (in two volumes)
	Italian Journey
	Maxims and Reflections
	Selected Verse
	The Sorrows of Young Werther
Jacob and Wilhelm Grimm	**Selected Tales**
E. T. A. Hoffmann	**Tales of Hoffmann**
Friedrich Hölderlin	**Selected Poems and Fragments**
Henrik Ibsen	**Brand**
	A Doll's House and Other Plays
	Ghosts and Other Plays
	Hedda Gabler and Other Plays
	The Master Builder and Other Plays
	Peer Gynt
Søren Kierkegaard	**Fear and Trembling**
	Papers and Journals
	The Sickness Unto Death
Georg Christoph Lichtenberg	**Aphorisms**
Karl Marx	**Capital** (in three volumes)
Karl Marx/Friedrich Engels	**The Communist Manifesto**
Friedrich Nietzsche	**The Birth of Tragedy**
	Beyond Good and Evil
	Ecce Homo
	Human, All Too Human
	Thus Spoke Zarathustra
Friedrich Schiller	**Mary Stuart**
	The Robbers/Wallenstein
